Dear God

Dear God

Dear God

Josephine Falla

Matador
9 Priory Business Park
Kibworth Beauchamp
Leicestershire LE8 0RX, UK
Tel: (+44) 116 279 2299
Fax: (+44) 116 279 2277
Email: books@troubador.co.uk
Web: www.troubador.co.uk/matador

ISBN 978 1780881 362

British Library Cataloguing in Publication Data.
A catalogue record for this book is available from the British Library.

Typeset in Bembo by Troubador Publishing Ltd

Matador is an imprint of Troubador Publishing Ltd

Printed in Great Britain by the MPG Books Group, Bodmin and King's Lynn

For David and Michael

CHAPTER 1

It was during one of his periodic bouts of smouldering resentment at the way his life had turned out that William Penfold first thought of emailing God. It seemed more modern than praying, somehow. More up to date. Anyway, he didn't want to pray. He wanted to protest. He'd been on this earth about 70 years or so, he thought, give or take. He wasn't quite sure of the exact length of time. The point was, he did not like the way he was living. It was not comfortable enough. Most of the time he was angry about things. He didn't want to be perpetually angry. He wanted serene comfort. He would tell the Lord about it all and see if He could put it right.

Informing the Lord about his situation by email meant deciding what the best address was. He gave the matter some thought. TheLord@cyberspace.com didn't seem right, somehow. Neither did theAlmighty@heaven.org.uk; he had a sudden feeling that 'orgs' were something to do with websites, not emails. Besides, who was to say that God resided in the UK? He could be any nationality, surely? Or, even more likely, not of any nationality. Nor of any particular gender, either.

That idea startled him. He paused to consider if he wanted anything to do with a female god. On the whole, he thought, no. Having a woman in charge might take him back to the days when. On the other hand, if that was what he had to deal with, he had no choice. He would have to assume it was a male god unless proved wrong. So what did he want to deal with?

He wanted to deal with the Boss. The Boss of all Bosses. Were there any other gods? There were certainly other religions, other beliefs, each of which was convinced that it was THE one. Each belief had its own god. There must be dozens of gods. Might be, anyway. Well, he couldn't send emails to all of them, on the off chance.

In the end, he settled for topgod@theuniverse.com. It seemed to cover all situations. He took a slow, leisurely drink, sat back in his chair and considered what he wanted to say. The anger was still bubbling inside him but was partially suppressed on account of the need to consider the correct choice of words. Words that would convey his sense of fury and despair. Words that would spur the Almighty to act in a compassionate and helpful way. Eventually, he typed:

Dear God
You useless bloody waste of space – why don't you help me? I can't stand any more and what the fuck do you do? Nothing, sod all!
William Penfold

He took another swift drink and considered what he had written. He wasn't pleased with it. It could be improved. He gave it some thought, then altered it to:

Dear God
You useless bloody waste of space – why don't You help me? I
can't stand any more and what the fuck do You do? Nothing, sod all!
William Penfold
Manager

He read it again. The capital letters definitely gave it a more respectful tone. He was surprised to see that he had added 'Manager' to his name. He had forgotten that. That belonged to the days when. He couldn't remember, however, what he had been 'manager' of. But it didn't matter.

He clicked on Send and set off for the pub. There he met up with Jimmy Donovan; they downed a few pints, at first in a convivial mood. As the evening progressed they became more morose. Jimmy said he knew where they could get some really good stuff that would cheer them up but they would need money. Real money. Neither of them had more than the price of a few more pints. William became inwardly angry again. He left in a bad mood and set off towards his home, mumbling and swaying slightly. As he turned into his street, a downwardly mobile row of rather grubby terraced houses, he saw his nextdoor neighbour, Mrs. Brenner, on her doorstep, letting in her cat.

"Evening," he said, "cat's alright then." Why he said this, he didn't know. He loathed Mrs. Brenner. And her cat. Interfering old biddy.

"Drunk again, then, Mr Penfold."

"Mind your own bloody business."

Sod her. Sod the lot of 'em. He got into his home, searched round for something to drink and found an already-opened can of lager which still had some left inside. He sat down in front of the telly. *Question Time*. It must be Thursday. Bunch of tosspots arguing over something or other. Incomprehensible. He switched channels but found nothing remotely watchable. The computer. He'd do something on the computer. If it still worked. He'd find an interesting website to look at. He lurched, stumbling, towards his PC and half fell into his chair in front of it. He opened his email programme.

Christ! There was a reply from God!

God had sent him a reply!

Some stupid bugger from Google! Must be. Someone who was going to fine him for something or other.

All the same, he'd better open it. He found himself curiously apprehensive. There seemed to be a lot of an enveloping darkness around him and the bright screen seemed to be compelling him to absorb its message.

He clicked on 'Open'. The message read:

What do you think is your problem?

That was all. No 'Dear William', no 'Regards, God'. Just 'What do you think is your problem?' He felt the fury well up inside him. Of all the stupid, patronising, brainless cretins – what an answer! If God didn't know what the problem was, who did?

Angrily, he pressed File and then Print. He wanted to see this email, see it in all its rudeness, study it to work out its origin. Only then did he remember that he did not have a printer. Why he did not have one he did not know. But he didn't. The email was there, but he could not print it. His anger grew, fuelled by frustration.

He needed a drink. Boy, did he need a drink! The lager was finished. He swayed along the passage to the kitchen and began hunting for something, anything, to drink. Amidst all the assorted piles of empty cans and bottles, at the back of a cupboard, he was in luck. One more can of lager. Looking round, he saw a pile of various pills behind the toaster. He could not remember what they were for or when he was supposed to take them, but he knew they were important. Blue ones, he thought. I have to have two blue ones, I remember that. And three of those little white ones. He opened a packet of capsules. They were pink. Damn.

Finally he took one of the pink ones and two white ones. I'll have the blue later on, he thought. When I've found them.

There was a half-open packet of digestive biscuits on the table, so he took those back with him to the sitting room. Right. Now, what to say to God? The cheek of it! 'What do you think your problem is?'

Well, what was his problem? He paused. Was it that he couldn't remember what he had been manager of? Was it that he didn't seem to be having a comfortable sort of life? Was it that he just didn't have the sort of drink he wanted? He didn't really care for all this beer and lager. He knew that but he couldn't afford anything better.

So was his problem drink? Was that it?

No. He liked drink. That wasn't his problem. His problem was that he couldn't afford it. He didn't have enough money. *That* was his problem.

Pleased at having solved the question posed to him on the email, he constructed his reply.

My problem is obvious. I haven't got enough money, have I? Why can't You do something about it? And why don't You do something about Mrs. Brenner while You're at it? Deck Mrs. B., she's a nasty old cow.

William Penfold
Administrative Manager

Triumphantly, he pressed Send.

Then he lay down on the sofa and fell asleep. In the middle of the night he woke up and was amazed to remember that he had put 'Administrative' in front of 'Manager'. What on earth did that mean? What *was* an administrative manager? Puzzling over this he fell asleep again.

Next day dawned bright and sunny, but that was lost on William, as he didn't struggle off the sofa until after ten-thirty. He tottered to the toilet, which fortunately was downstairs, and from there to the kitchen. There was very little to eat in the kitchen and, more importantly, nothing to drink. Nothing that he wanted to drink, anyway. Even the milk smelt a bit funny. No tea then. No coffee. No proper drink. A few slices of bread. Small tin of beans? Nah. Most of the label had come off, but the bit that was left didn't look like beans. He would have to go to the shop, the mini-market, two streets away.

Money. Had he got enough? A hasty search revealed a five pound note and four one pound coins. That was it. He tried to remember when the Social people would call. They usually sorted out his money. Sometimes he wrote down when they said they were coming. Sometimes they wrote and told him, gave him dates, but he almost always threw those away. He didn't know. He would have to live on the fiver and the coins until they came. Anyway, the electricity was working. Must be. He'd had an email from God, hadn't he? Wait till he told Jimmy Donovan! He'd piss himself laughing.

No. No, definitely not. He must not tell Jimmy or anybody else anything at all about the email. Especially the social workers. They would – what was the word? – they would section him. Again. They would take him away to that place with red curtains, where they hadn't let him out and tried to stop him drinking and tried to get him to talk about the time when. Well, he wasn't going to talk about the time when, so there. They were always asking him about voices, but he didn't hear any voices, he kept telling them all. No voices. Now emails – different thing altogether. But this was private. This was real.

CHAPTER 2

He set off, banging his front door firmly behind him. Outside, an ambulance was parked. He held on to the doorpost in sudden terror. Had they come for him? So quickly? But no – two ambulance men were rolling a stretcher out of Mrs. Brenner's. She was on the stretcher, pale and unconscious, with a livid mottled bruise on her forehead.

"What's the matter with her?" he asked the men.

"Dunno at this stage. She's got a bad bruise on her head. Must have fallen and hit herself on something."

"Struck by a thunderbolt, I expect," he muttered, as he watched the ambulance drive off.

The implication of what he had just said didn't sink in straightaway but when it did he felt his legs begin to crumble beneath him. Was this God's doing? And, if so, was it because he, William Penfold, had requested it?

Surely not! Surely the Almighty would not deliberately floor Mrs. B. just because he had suggested – no, demanded – it? All the same, it was a funny sort of coincidence.

He turned and went back into his own house. He stared at

the computer. Another email, he would send another email. After much thought he typed:

What did You do that for? I didn't really mean for the stupid old bat to get hurt like that. What I want is money.
William Penfold
Administrative Manager

Firmly, he pressed Send. For some time he continued to stare at the screen; then he hauled himself to his feet and wandered along to the kitchen again, but there was still nothing much to eat or drink. Lots of empty cans and bottles, all over the place, but no new, full ones. Opening one of the cupboards proved lucky, though, for he found three slices of bread at the back which didn't smell too bad. He put two of them into the toaster, which reminded him of the pills he hadn't taken, as they were stacked in a heap behind it. This time he found and took two of the blue ones, and a white one, just to be on the safe side. There was a scraping of marge, to go with the toast, and just water to drink. Well, better than nothing. But not much.

Time to go shopping. He set off along the passage, past the toilet, and paused at the doorway of the sitting room. He found he could not resist going closer to the computer. Slowly, almost in a trance, he reached forward and opened the email programme.

There was a reply. Another missive from the Top Guy. Or Gal.

Hand shaking he clicked on Open. It said:

Mrs. Brenner needs help.

Bloody hell! *She* needs help! *I* need help. How can I help her? Why should I anyway? I don't even know what hospital she's in, do I?

Shopping. Do some shopping. Get some food. Get something to drink. He set off briskly, in a determined mood. Outside his front door, in front of the step, was a large ginger cat.

Mrs. Brenner's.

Animal and man regarded each other. Christ, was this what the Top Guy meant? Was he supposed to look after the moggy till the old bat came home? His heart sank. He didn't want – what didn't he want? He didn't want the responsibility. He couldn't look after himself – he knew that – he hadn't done any looking after anybody or anything since the time when and he sure as hell didn't want to be bothered right now with a flaming cat.

Damn and blast it. He hadn't got money for himself, never mind a cat.

He turned to close the front door firmly but the cat was quick. It was inside before he had a chance to kick it out of the way.

He shrugged and turned towards the shops. In the mini-market he bought milk and bread and a tin of beans. He was about to reach for a can of lager when he thought of the wretched cat. What did cats eat? Had he ever had a cat? As usual he couldn't remember. Tinned mice perhaps? Eventually, he found the pet food section and bought the largest, cheapest can of cat food he could see. There was enough left over for two bottles of cheap beer. He set off back home, muttering curses to himself about the arrival of the cat into his daily routine.

Once home, he made himself a coffee and a piece of toast and sat down in front of the telly. He had forgotten about the cat, but it appeared from nowhere and started to rub itself against his trousers.

Hell's bells, it wants food, he thought. Muttering to himself he rose unsteadily to his feet and swayed towards the kitchen. There he managed, after a struggle, to open the tin of cat food and dished out a portion of it into a saucer. The cat fell on it instantly. After a little thought, he filled another saucer with a little milk. There. That was the animal settled.

He watched it finish the food and have a sip or two of the milk, then he opened the back door wide and invited his unwelcome guest to leave. The cat took one look, turned, fled down the passageway from the kitchen and shot upstairs.

Blast and bugger it, it's gone upstairs. He hadn't been upstairs for ages. He found he could manage perfectly well without the trouble and worry of getting up and down the stairs. He didn't want the cat up there. If he let it go up there it would make a home up there, and bring its friends in.

He pondered the situation. Eventually he decided that he'd have to get the cat down and he started on the precarious and wobbly business of ascending the stairs. About 10 minutes later he reached the top. There were three rooms upstairs – the main front bedroom, a smaller one at the back and a tiny bathroom, which he never used these days. He stumbled into the main bedroom. It contained a double bed with rumpled bed clothes, which obviously hadn't been slept in for ages. There was an old battered dressing table and an old battered wardrobe, whose door was swinging open. He lurched forward to close the door – and the cat leapt out with a rush. "Damn thing," he muttered. As he touched the door he caught a glimpse of a jacket inside the wardrobe, hanging on a battered coat hanger. Suddenly interested, he tore the jacket off the hanger, sat on the bed and inspected the garment.

Well, it must be his. He didn't recognise it. But it was his house, wasn't it? He stared at it closely. It was good quality. It reminded him of the days when. He felt in all the pockets. In the inside breast pocket he found a wallet. In the wallet he found a credit card in the name of W. Penfold. And some money. Actual money! Notes and coins. Excitedly he added it up. £76.84 pence! It was his. Must be his.

He put the jacket on. He felt different. A different sort of man. The sort of man who had a credit card, who had money in his pocket, who wore a jacket. As in the days when.

He stood up, still unsteady. Got to get down the stairs. Worse going down than coming up. Gingerly, he began the descent. God, he needed a drink. As he negotiated the last step, he realised that he didn't know where the cat was. It might still be up there. Well sod it, it would have to stay there. He wasn't going up there again for any fuckin' moggy.

The door to the sitting room was open and the computer faced him. So was this the work of the Almighty? He, William Penfold, had asked for money and the Top Man had told him to help Mrs. Brenner. Which he had done, by feeding her cat. And through the cat he had found money. Well, some anyway. So now what?

This required thought. Thought required drink. He turned towards the kitchen and opened a bottle of beer. Dimly, he remembered the pills and took two of the first ones he opened. He turned back towards the sitting room and fell onto the sofa, where he settled down for a drink and sleep. He eyed the computer and wondered if he should send a 'thank you' email to God but decided he couldn't be bothered at the moment. He put his feet up, drank the beer and dozed off. The afternoon drifted on.

When he woke up, he found he had a large ginger cat sprawled across his lap. Automatically he began to stroke it. It purred and stretched a little.

He started to think about the money. About what he could do with it. He could buy some drink. Proper drink. What was 'proper drink'? Vaguely he remembered wine. And spirits. Stuff like that. He'd liked it once, in the days when, he was sure. Might be a tad difficult now. You had to have – what was it now? – oh, yes. Mixers. And glasses. Different shaped glasses. He wondered if he had any glasses. Maybe in the top cupboard in the kitchen.

He could buy some food. He hadn't eaten anything you could call a decent meal for ages. What sort of food? Something that either didn't need cooking or was already cooked. A Chinese takeaway. Or Indian. Fish and chips. He could buy some proper stores. Eggs and things. Eggs were easy. Bacon. Rice pudding. Cheese. Thinking about food almost made him hungry. But not quite. What he was was thirsty.

A further thought occurred to him. This credit card. He forced his mind to concentrate. Credit cards. Was it still usable? Didn't they stop being valid or something, after a certain time? When had he last used it, and paid the bill? He didn't have the least idea. He didn't have any statements or anything. If they'd sent him one he'd thrown it away. And what was the other thing you needed? He couldn't remember. Something to do with needles. Something sharp. No, it was gone.

Laboriously he stood up, tipping the cat on to the floor as he did so. "Come on, Ginger, let's see what's in the kitchen." The sound of his voice, talking to a cat, alarmed him. I shall have to watch it, he thought, might be going a bit soft in the head. They set off down the passage together. Once in the kitchen, he found the other bottle of beer and opened it. Then he fixed himself some beans on toast. Using the toaster reminded him of the pills stacked behind it and he took one of everything. He gave the cat some more of the tin he had bought earlier. Again, he opened the back door, and this time the cat went out.

"Well, that's him sorted," he muttered, and went back to the sitting room. There he sat on the sofa and again reviewed the situation. He was still wearing the jacket and this led him to consider his wardrobe. The trousers, he decided, were filthy. So was the rest of his clothes. When had he last had a good wash? There was no answer to that and he fell to thinking about the credit card. If it was still valid he could use it on the internet! If it wasn't, the internet would tell him. So it was worth a try, at least.

Where did his money come from? He pondered this. Every so often the Social people visited him and they took him off to – where? The post office? Or somewhere else, he forgot where. He signed something and there was money, he knew that. Then they went with him to the mini-market and he bought things. Beans and stuff. Usually, as now, by the time they came again he had run out of all the stuff he had bought and was on his last drop of drink, last crumb of bread. And they supervised him doing laundry in the launderette. They had a quick look round the house, checked the electricity and so on.

Sometimes they tried to make him talk about the past, about the days when. But he wasn't having that. No way. They took him to the doctor's if he needed an appointment; they checked on his pills and tried to establish if he had been taking the right ones at the right time. And they talked about his drink problem. They didn't seem to realise he didn't have a drink problem. He had a pay-for-it problem – and God had helped him out with that. And they sorted out his post, if he had any.

He was back to the question of the credit card. He went to the computer and carefully ignored his email programme. He brought up his access to the internet. Now what?

He could order a big crate of champagne. A new enormous television. A Rolex watch. But it was no good. He didn't want these things. He began a surfing expedition, switching from website to website, fascinated by all the things he could order and have delivered within a week. Finally, he made a choice. Two – no, three, no, four choices, in fact.

On a large, multi-purpose site, he ordered a bright red snazzy little mobility scooter, which cost £4,000. It was intended for disabled people and had all possible additional gadgets, horn, mirrors, baskets, side flaps etc. Marvellous,he thought. I can't walk much these days – I'll whizz round to the mini-market with this. Maybe go even further – it says it will go 25 miles before it conks out. I could take all my laundry round myself to the launderette in it and tell those Social Service people to get lost. On further reading he became a bit concerned about the charging- up procedure – he didn't have a garage. But on reflection he could get it into the kitchen, out through the back door, and out of the garden into the alleyway at the back. He could plug it in in the kitchen.

He then thought of the cat. He would buy it a nice basket. He had got over his resentment at the cat's intrusion into his life, seeing as how it had introduced him, in a way, to some real money. He would give it a treat.

He discovered the Menswear section. There were some startling pale cream summer trousers, with an unexpected red stripe. I like those, he thought. So he added them to the list.

Finally he ordered himself a large golfing umbrella. He often got wet going round to the pub or the mini-market. It would be very sensible and practical. It was very cheerful; it was bright red with yellow and green stripes.

He then pressed the Proceed to the Check Out button on the website. He took a last swig of the beer as he filled in the details of his name, address and credit card, ordering everything to be delivered Express, which cost a lot more, he noticed, then with a deep, anxious breath, he clicked on Submit.

The wait seemed interminable. He suddenly thought that he did not know what his spending limit was on the card. Well, too late now.

The next page flashed up.

Your Purchase was Successful.

Delivery within two days. A confirmation email was being sent. Fantastic! He sat back in his chair and beamed with satisfaction.

CHAPTER 3

Now, what about God? With a certain amount of nervous bravado he opened up his email programme. He had to tell Him what he'd done and he suspected He might be more than a bit annoyed, being a bit hot on the morality thing. Still, he hadn't bought lots of drink, just practical things. It was just that he couldn't actually pay for them.

There was no email from God, so he wrote one to send off. After much thought, he put:

What did You do that for? I didn't really mean for the stupid old bat to get hurt like that. But thank you anyway for the money which is what I really want.
William Penfold
Administrative Manager

He wondered if he had struck the right tone. Was it grateful enough? And he was stealing, in a way, he couldn't disguise that fact. Eventually he added 'Best Wishes', which sort of softened it up a bit.

Just as he finished writing the email, he received the confirmation email from the big store where he had ordered all his stuff. He had ordered everything Express; it was all coming within the next two days, for which he had paid quite a lot extra. Still, it was all very satisfactory, as he didn't often have very much to look forward to.

There was time to go round to the mini-market before his evening session with Jimmy. When he opened the front door, the cat was just crossing the road towards his house; it began to race towards the front door and was nearly run over by a car. That worried him. Somehow the cat must be persuaded not to go out the front. The question bothered him all the way to the mini-market. Once he was there he bought some butter, milk, sausages, cereal and, of course, several cans of lager. On impulse he bought a whole cooked chicken, still warm. He saw some men's socks and bought three pairs of those, as the ones he was wearing had holes in them. They were also rather dirty, but it was the holes he objected to. He also saw, next to the socks, an assortment of baseball caps, in bright colours. He bought a yellow one.

Armed with his purchases, he paid at the check-out desk. Paid with real money! The girl, who recognised him, looked at him somewhat amazed, but said nothing. He hadn't realised how heavy all his things would be. It would be good to have that motorised buggy thing. He tried to estimate if he could get it into the shop and decided it would be rather tricky. Maybe he could go to the supermarket further down the road. He wasn't allowed in there, strictly speaking, after the incident involving the tomatoes and the cans of soup, when he had been accused of shoplifting and there had been a scene and the

Social people had had to come round and sort it out. But perhaps they wouldn't recognise him with his buggy. And the cap. You could go in there actually on a buggy; he had seen people inside, crashing unsteadily round the aisles. He'd try that, then.

Eventually he got home. The cat was waiting for him on the step. He had a splendid meal of chicken, bread and butter and lager. He'd forgotten to get anything for pudding, but the lager was good. He gave a chicken leg to the cat, who was delighted with it, and they munched away happily in the sitting room before the television, which had a panel game show on. He managed to understand it for once and was scathing about the contestants. "Brain dead!" he confided to the cat.

The problem about the cat being nearly run over returned to him. If he could persuade it to always come in through the back door, not the front, perhaps it would be easier. He thought about buying a cat flap but he had no idea how you would install it. Eventually he went out to the garden at the back, which was a small piece of untended, rubbish-strewn wilderness with a derelict shed at the bottom, near the back gate, which led into the alleyway at the back of the houses. He studied the door and windows at the back of the house. The downstairs toilet had a very small window, he noticed. Not large enough for a burglar to get through. Amidst the rubbish, he found a plank of wood, which he leant against the wall beneath the window. Then he went inside and opened the toilet window.

He brought the cat outside, protesting and wriggling, and tried to get it to walk up the plank and in through the window. It took several attempts but in the end the cat did manage it.

This was a major achievement and he and the cat celebrated with another bit of chicken. When he left he put the cat out into the garden and told it to stay there.

It had been a highly successful day and he set off for the pub with almost a spring in his step, except that he lurched a bit at the end of the road, by the traffic lights. However, Jimmy wasn't in the pub, and his attempts at conversation with other people were met with a distinct lack of enthusiasm. After a few pints he decided to turn in, as he felt tired anyway.

When he got home, he discovered that the cat had remembered his way in and had discovered the sausages; it was in the sitting room chewing its way through one on the rug in front of the telly. Damn animal! But he was secretly quite proud of it. He looked nervously at the computer. It was no use. He would have to see if there was an email for him from Top God.

There was. It said:

Mrs. Brenner needs further TLC.

That was all. Nothing about his money problems. Nothing about having been the originator of Mrs Brenner's crack on the head. Just a curious directive about the old bat's state. Why and how he, William Penfold, was supposed to assist her was a mystery.

Disappointed, angry and fed up, he and the cat settled down for the night on the sofa. William's mind was buzzing, swirling with more-than-half-forgotten events from the past and the present, all mixed up. Was he a write off? A man who had once been an administrative manager – whatever that was – who had had, perhaps, a home, a car, a future. Maybe even a family.

What had turned him into this seedy, drunken, shambolic shadow of a man? A man in filthy trousers, with a run-down garden and no money? A man who ordered things he could not possibly pay for? A man who lived downstairs because he was too idle and too drunk half the time to climb up to the bathroom or front bedroom?

As none of these questions could be answered, he wondered briefly about his mother. He hadn't thought about his parents for months. There was an indistinct memory of warmth and an enveloping tenderness; she always gave him 'TLC', as Top God phrased it in his email.

But these emails were winding him up, like the Social people tried to do, he decided, making him confront things he didn't wish to remember.

He suddenly perceived the acute difference between 'didn't wish to' and 'couldn't'.

Sod 'em all. He would have another little drink or two and go to sleep. So he did.

Next day dawned grey and showery. The cat was up and about early, climbing through the toilet window to the wider world outside, taking another sausage with it. William was woken by the postman knocking on the door loudly. Three parcels. One contained a pair of trousers, cream with the red stripe, bright, clean and new. The next one contained a long and colourful umbrella. He couldn't remember ordering an umbrella at all, but it seemed very sensible. It also seemed like a present, as he had no recollection of buying it. The third item was somewhat problematic. He had meant to get the cat a nice basket to sleep in but it appeared he had ordered a carrying basket instead, the type you saw people taking their pets to the vet's in. It was well-made and had a little cover, with a hole for the handle, so as not to upset the animal.

Well, it would have to sleep in that; just as good as a sleeping basket, provided you didn't click the front bars up.

He liked the look of the trousers but a thought occurred to him. If his current trousers were dirty, could he put on clean ones without having a shower or bath first? It was a thorny question. There was hot water, he knew. Would there be enough for an all-over job? Did he have any clean underwear? Or a shirt of some description?

Where was all this leading him? He had a presentiment of impending change, which was alarming. But the trousers did look inviting. He went to the chest of drawers in the far corner of the room. Yes, two pairs of underpants and a tee shirt which was a bit grey but not as dirty as the one he had on. Socks – he'd bought some yesterday. Must be in the kitchen.

Bit by bit he organised himself. Having a shower involved climbing the stairs again. He was accustomed to washing himself in the sink in the kitchen. Still, he persevered and managed at last to get up the stairs and into the bathroom. The shower worked, rather half-heartedly, as if very surprised to be asked to do anything at all and the water was hottish. He didn't have any soap though. He still had an electric razor which he used sporadically and did so this morning.

He cooked himself two sausages of the ones that were left and ate them with some bread and a can of lager. His mind felt clear and lucid, although not filled with any useful information, except that he needed to buy some soap and do some laundry. He wondered when the motor scooter would arrive. The anticipation was exciting.

CHAPTER 4

In the early afternoon there was a knock at the door. It was a large van and a man was offloading a motorised scooter from the back. The cat had come in by now and stood by him to watch the proceedings.

"Motor Scooter for Penfold," said the man, with a sheet for him to sign. "Where d'you want it, mate?"

"In the kitchen," said William.

"Gawd," said the delivery man.

William opened the front door wide and the man took the vehicle along the passage to the kitchen. "Won't go in there, mate," said the man. "Not enough room."

William thought for a bit, then opened the back door, took out the kitchen table and put it in the garden. "Plenty of room now," he said.

"Right," said the man, "charge it up for eight hours. Manual of instructions. Extras all in this package. Dead easy. Don't go up and down kerbs, you'll do it in. Don't drive it in a strong wind."

"Thank you," said William, and the man was gone.

William plugged it in and left it to charge itself up, taking the manual and a can of lager with him into the sitting room. It looked a wonderful vehicle. It would give him freedom – well, at least 25 miles of freedom. Marvellous.

After studying the instructions, during which he fell asleep, he woke up to find the cat again on top of him, asleep. Carefully he lifted the animal into the open cat basket, where it seemed to be comfortable and content.

"We need some more shopping," he said. "Stuff like soap and puddings. And more sausages," he said with a smile.

He could not remember when he had last smiled. Actually it hadn't been long ago, when he had realised the credit card was still valid. All the same, it disturbed him. What was happening to him? Not enough drink. Not enough to blot it all out. Not strong enough. People laughed at him because he shuffled along. He was sure of that. They would stop that now because, with him on a buggy, they would have to get out of the way. Tomorrow. And he would smile at them instead of scowling. Or swearing. People didn't like swearing, although they did it all the time themselves. The man at the papershop had told him "there's too much bleedin' bad language these days". He'd go round there now and try smiling. He'd buy a paper. Normal thing to do. Those Social people, they were always asking him who the Prime Minister was. As if he cared. He'd have known alright, in the days when. But he didn't follow it all now. Why did they ask him, a perfect stranger? Why didn't they know who it was? Ridiculous. They shouldn't have ignorant people like that in responsible jobs, not knowing who the Prime Minister was.

He suddenly thought, maybe they're trying to make out

I'm a bit crazy. I'd better get a paper and find out who it is. They're not going to catch me like that. He had worked himself up into a temper now and set off in something of a rage. He put on his new yellow cap as he went out and left the cat in the sitting room. Dimly he realised that with the new entrance and exit arrangements for the cat he would have to clear up the kitchen and put the food away. Bloody animal.

In the newsagent's he bought the nearest paper to hand, which dealt with some juicy scandal on the front page. "You live next door to Mrs. Brenner, don't you?" said the newsagent.

"Yes, why?" said William, still in a belligerent mood.

"Poor lady's in St Anne's Hospital," said the man. "Not doing too well. Had a nasty fall."

William thought for a second or two. *Mrs Brenner needs further TLC* floated across his mind. "St. Anne's you say?"

"Yes."

Back in the house he went to see his new possession. He sat on it, felt all the instrumentation, longed to take it out. Tomorrow, he thought. Tomorrow. He couldn't wait for tomorrow. When was the last time he had looked forward to tomorrow?

The evening passed well enough. Jimmy expressed amazement at his cream trousers, his jacket and yellow baseball cap. They had a couple of pints to celebrate his smart appearance. Then another two to make sure they knew what was what, as Jimmy put it, and a further three or four just to round things off. By the time he got back home William was well away. He went into the sitting room and collapsed on to the sofa. "Must do something about the garden," he announced to an uninterested cat. "Must make a shopping list. Have you had another bloody sausage?" Then he fell asleep and did not wake up until half-past nine the next morning.

When he woke up he rolled off the sofa and shook his head to clear it, which it didn't do. In the kitchen, he was amazed to see the red buggy and no sign of his table but gradually his memory came back. He found some food and milk for the cat, who was by now a fixture, it seemed. He had some toast and an assortment of pills, as he didn't remember having had any for a while. He had a drink.

Right. Now for it. He unplugged the machine and folded the wire back into the slot at the back. He decided to go out the back way, so opened the door, sat on the buggy and switched it on. He put it into gear and the machine moved forward, through the doorway. Oh, the joy of movement! Wonderful feeling. Then he hit the table.

He managed to stop. Now what? He got off and moved the table and considered the situation. It was raining. He was going to get very, very wet. Oh no he wasn't. He remembered the umbrella. He studied the buggy. There were two spring slots on the side, intended to carry walking sticks. If he could twist one of them to hold the umbrella upright, he would be fine. He went back into the house and fetched the umbrella. After a few minutes, struggling, he had got the umbrella upright and held firmly. He opened it up. It was large, he had to admit, but it would shield him well from the rain. It was not centrally placed above the driving seat but a foot or two to the right, of course, but it was big enough to shelter him adequately. He also put on his baseball cap. He put a couple of bottles of beer into the small container at the front.

It was then that he had his idea. If he were to go to St.

Anne's, which was only about a mile away, he could visit Mrs. Brenner. She might not be too pleased to see him, or he to see her, but there again, he would have done his best. And – here was the really, really splendid thing – he could take the cat with him. If he could get the cat into the carrying basket and close it, and put the cloth over it, and if it would fit into the big basket at the back of the buggy, then he would be well sorted! She would really like that, he thought.

This he managed to do. The cat squawked a fair bit when he closed the front up but when he put the cloth over it, it went quiet. It slotted into the basket at the back of the machine perfectly. With great pride and a degree of panache he set off.

He didn't go on the pavement. He felt he was better off on the actual road and the drivers of the other cars on the road, seeing a bright red machine apparently topped by a large multi-coloured mushroom, were keen to give him a wide berth. The cat was silent and William, although he had not had a shower, nor even a wash, felt smart and well-dressed in his new cream trousers and yellow baseball cap.

"We'll call at the supermarket on the way back," he said over his shoulder.

CHAPTER 5

Arriving at the hospital William was unable to find a parking space. Angrily he drove round and round until, eventually, he slotted into a space marked 'Senior Consultant'. Then there was the question of whether to leave the umbrella up on the motorised scooter, an invitation to thieves, or to protect himself by removing it from the machine and using it against the rain. It was difficult to remove but he at last did so and he set off for the main entrance, taking with him a bottle of beer in his trouser pocket and the cat basket, still covered by the carrying cloth. In the other hand he carried the still-open umbrella, which had the effect of making it impossible to see where he was going. He caused a certain amount of justifiable annoyance amongst the many visitors to the hospital as he bumped into them, prodding them with the spokes of his gaudy protector. Once in the entrance hall, he was then faced with a problem he hadn't thought of. Which ward was she in?

Some people were sitting at a table near the back wall of the hall. They looked rather bored and he decided to enlist their help as it might cheer them up a bit if he gave them something to do.

"Where is she?" he demanded, in a tone which implied that they had done something untoward with the lady.

"Where is who?" asked one of them, in surprise at the apparition before him.

"Mrs. Brenner, of course."

"What is she in the hospital for?" This from another gentleman, also somewhat bemused.

"Because she's ill, of course," snapped William, waving the umbrella wildly. The baseball cap was slipping sideways but he did not have a free hand to regulate it. "She's got a bruise on her head," he added, remembering her appearance when he last saw her. "I think God did it, but it was probably a mistake," he added, uncomfortably.

They went into an uneasy huddle. "Could she be in Acute Admissions?" one of them suggested..

"Try Acute Admissions," they said, anxious, as he had mentioned God, for him to go away. "Up those stairs there, second floor, Springfield Ward."

"Right ho," said William. He spied a sign saying 'Lifts'.

"I think you might be more comfortable if you put the umbrella down," said the first man, kindly.

"I didn't come here to be comfortable," said William, and made for the lifts. In the lift he did not have a free hand to press the button for the second floor and he went up to the sixth floor, then came down to the fifth, then the third and was just able to persuade a tall official-looking gentleman that he wanted Acute Admissions. He seemed to agree that it was quite likely that William wanted Acute Admissions, and he bundled him out on the second floor, much to the relief of the group of trapped travellers in the lift, who had little room, confined as they were by William and his still-open umbrella.

On the second floor William found Springfield Ward and made his grand entrance. He was enjoying himself now. Everyone seemed to be against him but he was overcoming all obstacles. A nurse, scarcely believing what she was seeing, stopped in front of him.

"Hands," she said.

"Pardon?"

"Hands. You should wash your hands."

"Why?"

"Well, you just should. Health and Safety. Stop infection."

"I haven't got any infection," he said angrily. "I just want to see Mrs. Brenner."

"And you must put that umbrella down. It's dangerous and it's not raining in here."

"I like it up," he said, suddenly angry again. "Where does it say I can't have my umbrella up? It's ready for when I go outside."

The nurse was now irritated and wanting to be well away from this nuisance of a visitor.

"Mrs. Brenner's in the side room," she said. "Don't disturb her too much. She needs rest and quiet." He had struck lucky. She was here, in the side room.

He went in. Mrs. Brenner was sitting up in bed, propped up by two big pillows, gazing mournfully into space.

"William Penfold!" she exclaimed in utter astonishment. "What on earth are you doing here?"

"I've come to see how you are," he said. "After you got whacked on the head," he added.

"I didn't get whacked," she said. "I fell down in the kitchen. Tripped over the cat."

"Well, whatever," he said. "I've brought you something."

She stared at him. Never in her life could she have imagined her next door neighbour in such an outfit, nor indeed could she ever have imagined him making any sort of journey to see her. And what was he doing with a large umbrella and carrying something in his hand. What on earth was it?

He put the cat basket on the bed and placed the umbrella, still open, on the floor. He lifted the cloth on the basket and declared, with great pride, "Here's your cat come to see you."

"Oh my God," said Mrs. Brenner. "Oh my God, it's Sandy, it's my cat. I've been so worried, oh, dear oh dear, I'm all overcome." She was talking and crying and shaking her hands about.

The cat began to yowl in a determined sort of way and William let down the front of the basket. It sprang out of its shelter and allowed Mrs. Brenner to stroke it. But when the door opened and the nurse came in bearing some medication and a blood pressure gadget it made a leap for the curtains and shot up them, swearing and yowling.

"See what you've done," said William angrily, as the nurse tried to get round the upturned umbrella on the floor. "You've upset it," he said.

Mrs. Brenner was crying and calling, "Sandy, Sandy, come down, good puss."

"Here," he said, "have a drink." He took the beer out of his pocket and placed it on her bedside table. "There, do you good. Don't worry over your cat, I'm looking after it."

The nurse was bewildered, caught between an open umbrella on the floor, a patient who was being offered beer by a weird man in a yellow baseball cap plus a terrified cat howling on the top of the curtain, and she dropped her little pot of medications. Pills rolled on the floor. "Don't drink that beer," she said, from beneath the umbrella, as she sought to pick up the errant tablets.

"Why shouldn't she?" inquired William angrily. "Too many people interfering with what people want to do."

"Nurse! Whatever are you doing?" The voice came from Authority, who had just entered the room to see what all the uproar was about. Authority was represented by the figure of a Sister; behind her came a doctor in a white coat who was carrying a sheaf of papers.

"Shut the door quick," said the nurse, "There's a cat in here."

"That's my Sandy," said Mrs. Brenner. "My friend Mr. Penfold brought him in to see me. He's very upset. With all this shouting. The cat, I mean. Very upset. Can't you get him down?"

William heard the reference to 'my friend Mr. Penfold' and was impressed. He had opened the bottle of beer that Mrs. Brenner had been ordered not to drink and was happily drinking it himself.

"I'll get it down," he said. He dragged the only chair towards the window and, perilously, stood on it to reach up to the still-howling animal. As this was a man who had found it difficult to climb up a normal set of stairs only a day ago, standing on a chair reaching outwards and upwards proved to be an impossible task. Feeling himself slide unstoppably off the chair he grabbed the curtains and the whole lot, curtains, cat, chair and man, came tumbling down in a confused heap onto the floor.

Sister, nurse, patient and doctor viewed the shambolic muddle of the side room with varying degrees of amazement and bewilderment.

"Is Sandy alright?" shouted Mrs. Brenner.

"Nurse, pick up those pills and close that umbrella," ordered the Sister.

"That gentleman may have hurt himself." This came from the doctor.

"I should think he probably has," said the Sister, in a tone which implied that that was her fervent wish.

A bright yellow baseball cap surfaced first, then an arm, the fingers of which clutched the neck of a struggling cat. Eventually William emerged from the pile of curtains, with a certain amount of controlled dignity, holding the cat in his arms. "Those curtains are dangerous. You should bloody well get them fixed."

He placed the cat in the carrying basket on the bed, snapped the front bars closed, slipped the covering cloth over it, gathered up his umbrella, still open as the nurse had not managed to close it, and turned to go.

"Been very nice to see you, Mrs. B. The cat's alright with me. He likes sausages. Excuse me," he said, making his way through the medical trio barring his way to the door.

"Don't you dare come back in here with that animal." Sister had found her voice.

"If Mrs. Brenner wants me to I shall certainly bring it

back," he declared. "You can't interfere with Mrs. Brenner's human rights."

"No, you can't," said Mrs Brenner, from the bed.

He could still hear them arguing about Mrs. Brenner's human rights as he turned towards the lift. The idea obviously appealed to her. Apart from her right to receive a visit from her cat she was also demanding new curtains. It was strange, he thought. Until now it not have occurred to him that Mrs. Brenner had any human rights, still less that he would have cared about defending them!

Eventually, he made it to the space where he had parked the motor scooter, which now had a large notice affixed to it, advising him not to park in this bay again and informing him of the hospital's policy on non-payment of parking fees. This he took off and placed on a Lexus in the next bay. It took some time to re-attach the umbrella to the buggy and even more time to find how to put the machine into reverse, as this was not a manoeuvre he had been called on to perform before. He managed it at length, only giving the Lexus a minor scrape in a couple of places as he did so, and set off homewards.

"Think we'll give the supermarket a miss," he said over his shoulder. "Try it tomorrow."

CHAPTER 6

Once home, he put the motor scooter into the kitchen, having first removed the umbrella, and let a relieved cat out of the basket at the back. To his surprise, he found that he had acquired some post, which lay on the mat in the hall. Taking a bottle of beer with him, he and the cat went into the front room to read his letters, seated together on the sofa.

The first letter was from his credit card company, which informed him that he owed £4,097 in total, or a minimum payment of £125, payable by the 3rd of next month.

"Well, they haven't lost any time, have they, Ginger? Or is your name Sandy?" He stared at the sheet of paper in disbelief. "What the hell do we do now then?" He tried to think of any way he could raise that sort of money; theft seemed the most likely but he didn't know anywhere he could steal it from. He had a sudden brainwave. He would have to declare himself bankrupt. That was it. Then they couldn't touch him. Problem solved. But that meant he would lose his possessions, wouldn't it? The scooter, the computer, all his possessions and possibly the house. He had no idea if he owned the house or not. It was all very bewildering and he became very angry about it all.

He took another swig of the bottle and opened the second letter. It was from the Social Services people, the ones who came to sort out his money and laundry and medications and so on. They were going to come Wednesday. Today was Monday. At least he thought it was, but he could be wrong of course. No-one told him anything these days.

He thought about this. It was going to pose problems. He would have to put the motor scooter in the garden and bring the table inside. But what if it was raining? You couldn't leave the scooter out in the rain for hours on end, just because of them. Anger began to build up inside him. Interference again. He'd a good mind to tell them not to come. Could he do that, though? How could he explain where he'd got the scooter from?

He tried hard to remember where they took him to get the money out but it was no use. Some building society or other. Or bank. He couldn't afford to turn them away. He'd have to put the scooter in the garden and hope that they didn't see it.

The anger continued to build up inside him. All this interference. He'd go and do some shopping; he felt he needed action. Angrily he put on his new cap and went to collect the scooter. The cat had disappeared, presumably out of the toilet window. He manoeuvred the scooter out of the kitchen, locked the back door and set off. He still had a fair bit of money; he thought he would go to the bigger supermarket, where he could take the scooter inside. This time he didn't take the umbrella, which might have been awkward. The journey was uneventful and he was only hooted at twice.

The trouble started at the supermarket itself. He had amassed quite a large amount of shopping, putting it in the baskets at the front and back of his vehicle, from various aisles, before he was confronted by an irate manager.

"You can't bring that scooter in here," he roared, flailing his arms about in an effort to stop William, who was examining an artichoke with a puzzled expression on his face.

"I already have," said William. "I've seen other people in here on scooters."

"No you haven't," said the manager, "what you've seen is someone using our own Disability Assistance Vehicle – you can't bring in your own scooter."

"Why not?"

"Well, you just can't, that's why not. We'd have too many, and people would have accidents."

"How do you know people would have accidents?"

"They just would. Wait a minute – haven't I seen you in here before?" The manager's voice was rising as a dawning suspicion grew on him that he remembered something about a previous encounter involving tomatoes and a can of soup – a suspected shoplifting episode. The Social Services had become involved, he recalled, and it had all been noisy and unpleasant. And unproductive. They'd all shouted abuse at one another, or at least he and the man had, and he'd had to back down, although he was sure that something fishy had happened but he'd had to let the man go.

"Certainly I've been in here before. But not on my own scooter. And why isn't there any directions how to cook this thing?" William was waving the artichoke wildly.

"If you don't know how to cook it you shouldn't be buying it."

"So only people who know how to cook can avail themselves of your establishment?" William was becoming loquacious and pompous as the scene developed.

The manager, whose face was turning purple with fury, shouted, "Only people who can actually pay for what they select can come in here. And they can only come in here on foot," he added firmly.

"Supposing they want vehicular assistance?" said William.

"They can use the bloody scooter that belongs to the shop!" snapped the manager.

"There's no need to swear," said William, reprovingly.

"Pay for your purchases and get out," said the manager, making a huge effort to control his temper.

William did, making a sterling effort to align his scooter with the check-out counter top. The bill came to £45 and he just about made it. It took an inordinately long time to load stuff on to the counter and then reload on to his scooter, whilst the manager stood over him, announcing to all and sundry, "See, he can stand up perfectly well, he doesn't need a scooter, I knew it."

"Stop shouting at him," said a woman in the by now interested crowd around them. "You can need a scooter even if you can stand up."

"Yes," said another, glaring at the manager. "Little Hitler."

"Tell him how to cook an artichoke," said a third man. "He's bought one now."

"I expect he doesn't know," said William. "I bid you good afternoon, manager."

"Get out," was the reply.

William got out.

On the way home, he nearly had an accident with a white van, which appeared out of nowhere and almost collided with his scooter. In William's opinion, White Van Man had not been looking where he was going, had not seen William's signal, was driving too fast and was asking for trouble. White Van Man, on the other hand, said that William should not be on the road in the first place, he ought to be on the pavement, preferably with a keeper. He said that William was as blind as a bat and thick with it and if trouble was what he wanted he had come to the right place. William, noting that White Van Man was young and strong and twice his size, decided to defuse the situation by pretending he was deaf as well as stupid and drove off in a state of suppressed fury. He was not as keen on the scooter as he had been, as the incident had frightened him a little.

He was glad to get in and pour himself a can of lager. He started to unpack his purchases, but it was difficult as the table was outside. He went into the sitting room, where he was joined by the cat, and they sat on the sofa together, gloomily studying the television.

The sheet of paper from the credit card company was still there. "How the hell am I going to pay that, Ginger?" he muttered. He went to the kitchen, found some cat food underneath the artichoke and a pile of soap, and put out a saucer of food for Ginger (he had decided that Ginger suited him better than Sandy). He also put out some milk. He took another two cans of lager back into the living room and sat wearily down on the sofa again. It was nearly time to go to the pub, but he felt a little shaky. Might give it a miss tonight, he thought. That van driver! Ruining people's lives. He should have reported him.

A sudden thought struck him. God. God had got him into this mess. So God could get him out of it!

Apprehensively, he drew near to the computer. He brought up his email programme. There was another email. Bet it was from Him!

It was. It said:

Explore. Broaden your horizons.

He stared at it, stupidly. What on earth did that mean? Explore what? Why? He didn't go anywhere, except the pub. And the mini-market. And the supermarket. And the newsagent's, occasionally. St. Anne's Hospital, once. And the places the Social Services took him to. That was all. Quite enough for anyone. Why should he want to go anywhere else? All the trouble people got came from gallivanting about to Other Places. He hadn't gone to the trouble of buying a scooter just in order to Go Somewhere. He just wanted it to use when he needed to go somewhere...well, local.

When you Went Somewhere you had all the trouble of getting dressed for it, looking up the route, taking enough money with you. Like in the days when. A worry. And the scooter – he didn't have enough money for all this sort of thing. He couldn't even pay for it in the first place.

He was worried. The email had worried him. If God was going to continue sending him silly emails he wouldn't read them. He'd block them. There was a way of doing that, he was sure. But then Google would think he'd gone mad. Or BT or Yahoo. They'd gang up and make his life a misery. Anyway, to be fair, God's emails had been useful, so far. He'd got some money and a jacket, the cat and a baseball cap out of Him. And a cat basket and an umbrella. And the credit card and the scooter. If only he could pay the bill, he could go on using it. Oh hell.

He got up and went off to the kitchen again, fetched some more beer and settled down to have a muttering grumbling session. He had intended to try out the bed upstairs, he remembered, but he decided he wasn't going to be bothered. All this worry.

In this mood he fell asleep, with the cat on top of him, and slept till half past nine the next morning.

It was a lovely day. Was it today the Social Services people were due to come and disrupt him? No, today was Tuesday. He was sure of that. They'd be here tomorrow. Slyly trying to get him to remember the days when. Asking who the Prime Minister was. Taking him to get some money out. Doing the laundry run. Checking everything was working. Counting his tablets. Generally interfering with his lifestyle.

He shuffled along to the kitchen, found a can of lager and decided to put his shopping away. He made himself some breakfast, took two or three of his pills, which were still behind the toaster; the blue ones seemed to have gone down, perhaps he needed some more. He even washed up and made the kitchen tidy. Well, fairly tidy, if not very clean.

There was no sign of Ginger although the wrappings on the sausages had been torn somewhat and one appeared to be missing, so presumably he was alright. Among the shopping he discovered a leaflet that invited its readers to 'Visit Your Local Farm Shop and Nature Park'. This reminded him of God's email. Was this the sort of thing He meant? He had got hardly any money left so what was the point of going to a farm shop? Just a handful of small change. Still, he could go to the nature park. It didn't seem far to go. Westhamfield was a village on the road leading out of town, past the supermarket where he had had the altercation with that ridiculous manager yesterday. The memory of that scene came back to him with angry little jabs. Stupid man.

On impulse, he decided that yes, he would go. Cheer his life up a bit. Get a bit of fresh air.

CHAPTER 7

Carefully he washed and dressed himself, deciding to leave the shower upstairs until he felt a little stronger. His new trousers, jacket and yellow baseball cap made him feel smart; he had a shave and paused only to hesitate over whether to take the umbrella or not. He decided no, it looked sunny and bright. So he unlocked the back door and sat himself down on the scooter.

He wondered if he should give the pavement a go, instead of the road. The white van man had upset him, there was no denying it. He felt really rather vulnerable on his scooter. He stayed rather timidly on the pavement. Also, he felt rather cold, at least his hands did. So when he saw a lay-by ahead of him where there was a stall selling hot drinks and burgers and so on he decided to pull into it, parking behind a big lorry, and began to fish into his pocket to see if he had enough small change at least to buy a cup of tea. He had, and the hot tea was most welcome. He'd better wear gloves for this sort of outing, he thought. But perhaps not bring the cat. It mightn't like it and if it escaped he'd never get it back. Mrs. Brenner would be most upset.

At that point, whilst he was studying the traffic whizzing past, he heard a sickening sort of crunching noise. He turned and saw, to his horror, the huge truck, behind which he had so neatly and carefully parked, crushing and flattening his scooter, as if it was a child's toy! Someone alerted the driver and he was even now climbing out of his cab and running, pale and frantic, towards the back of his vehicle.

"Oh bloody 'ell!" gasped the driver, staring at the pulverised mess.

"It's mine," announced William. "See what you've done. You've ruined it."

"Oh my gawd," said the driver. "You alright?"

"Yes," said William. "No thanks to you, though. I could have been sitting on that when you started to reverse back on to me. You should look where you're going."

"I can't be expected to see you parked right out of my line of sight." The driver's voice was rising now; there was a hint of panic in his speech. Another man touched him on his sleeve, the same man who had alerted him to the disaster. They seemed to confer with each other, just out of William's earshot.

The driver turned to William. "How much?" he said.

"How much what?"

"How much is your scooter thing worth?"

"Four thousand pounds," he said. "I've only had it a few days," he added, mournfully.

The driver and his mate conferred again. "Right," said the driver, "I'll tell you what, Mr...."

"Penfold," said William. "William Penfold."

"Well, look here, William, I'm going to get a taxi to take you home and if you will kindly give me your address, I will come and see you early this evening and sort this lot out."

William was very dubious. He didn't know this lorry driver; didn't know his firm, it just said Bellamy Logistics on the side. No-one was going to sort this out, he felt. He'd got a bill for £125 or £4000+ total from the credit card company and now it was all ruined. And this man, driving his lorry in a stupid way, anxious to get on and deliver his logistics, whatever they were, had wrecked everything, nearly killed him in fact, just like that white van driver. He wanted to report him to somebody but suddenly he felt that the process of reporting, involving phone calls, and talking to the police – thoughts of the police made him shake up and think about the fact that he had ordered an expensive scooter without the wherewithal to pay for it. He really, really wanted to get home. He became rather shaky and confused.

The driver's friend got him another cup of tea and a burger. They found somewhere for him to sit down whilst he waited for the taxi and then returned to the scene of the crash, talking earnestly about how to get the scooter detached from the lorry's back end and what damage to the truck would then be revealed.

They paid the taxi for him, told him not to worry or do anything until the driver came to see him later that evening. He came home in style, which he rather enjoyed. Just like the days when, he thought, but didn't pursue the memories. He entered his house and was greeted by Ginger; he settled down on the sofa and considered whether to contact the police, after all. That would mean walking round to the police station as he hadn't got a phone. It sounded like a bit of a performance but he had more or less decided he should do that when he fell instantly asleep.

When he woke it was to the sound of the doorbell. He pushed Ginger off him and went to open the door. It was the driver. He hadn't got his lorry with him, just a plain ordinary car.

"I've come to sort it all out, Mr. Penfold," he said. "See, it's like this. If my company thinks I stopped off at a lay-by where, between you and me, I shouldn't have been in the first place, and then went and flattened an old boy's – sorry, an elderly gentleman's – scooter, even if he wasn't on it at the time, I reckon I'd lose my job. So it's in my interest and yours to settle up with you. I'm going to offer you £5,000 to say nothing about this to anybody. We, that's my mate and me, we'll clear it all up, clean the truck and get rid of the evidence – is it a deal?"

William said, "You can't repair it, then?"

"Beyond repair, mate."

"You said £5000?"

"Yeah. My job depends on it. And you've had a real shock and a lot of trouble – so I thought a bit extra like, well, sort of helpful for you."

The man was almost begging him, William thought. A wicked idea occurred to him – maybe he could push him up a bit! He toyed with this alluring prospect for a brief moment before something indefinable checked him. Perhaps something to do with having been a respected administrative manager at some point, perhaps more likely it was the sudden remembrance of his newly acquired electronic pen pal. If God had arranged for him to find his credit card and had allowed him to buy a scooter he couldn't afford, and had then staged an accident which would enable him to pay for it and have something left over, why, that was enough, wasn't it?

"Alright then," he said, trying to sound a bit reluctant.

"There's just one thing," said the driver. "I can only pay you in cash. That OK?"

"Yes," said William. The thought of having to go to his bank, wherever it was, with the Social Service people looking keenly over his shoulder, struck him as a very dodgy experience. Cash would be much better.

The driver looked relieved. He started to count out the money from a very large brown envelope on the coffee table in front of the sofa. It took a long time. When it was finished, it occurred to William to offer him a drink, which he accepted. He rather liked the new experience of having someone in his house, like a guest, and offering them a drink. Bit like in the days when. The driver left, stressing the need for secrecy, to which William gladly agreed, and William began to consider his options.

All in all it had been an exciting day. He found, to his amazement, that he didn't actually miss the scooter and decided not to replace it. It had been a bit beyond him. A bit dangerous. Maybe he would be safer in a car. But he pushed that thought away. What he had to decide now was how much he would pay the credit card company. £125? Or all of the £4000? Or something in between?

Even more importantly, he needed some supper. He felt he hadn't been down the pub for a while, but so much seemed to have happened it didn't seem important. The pub would always be there, when he wanted it.

Supper was a demanding experience. He had bought a ready meal for one but the directions for heating it up were in very tiny print, which sent him into one of his periodic rages, particularly as he couldn't find his glasses. He guessed it would take about five minutes to cook. Ginger was also demanding to be fed and rubbing himself against his trouser legs, which caused him to trip up. But the greatest problem was presented by the artichoke. It was bigger than he remembered it. Did you take the outside leaves off and then boil it? Or put it all in a big saucepan in one piece? He didn't think he had a saucepan big enough. Did you get the middle bits out, and were they edible, or the remaining outside bits? In the end, he lost his temper and boiled up what he could in the only saucepan he could find. Stupid vegetable. He resolved not to buy one again. He hadn't got any salt, which annoyed him further. Still, he added some baked beans, which made a passable job of it, fed Ginger, and sat down in the front room, in front of the television. He had a lager with it, in a glass which he had found at the back of a cupboard. Afterwards he had a steamed ginger pudding which he cooked in the microwave. The meal was not a great success, he had to admit, but he decided he would get the times right on his next venture.

Tomorrow 'They' were coming, he remembered. This time he would pay some attention and note where they took him to get his money. He didn't think he would have to go to the doctor's but he would have to go to the launderette. It would be lunchtime before he could get rid of them. Then what could he do? Pondering this he thought of the computer. Shouldn't he thank the Top God for everything? And tell Him that he would pay for it all? He wouldn't mess about with paying a little bit here and there. He'd pay for everything, now he'd got some money, like sensible people did. Like he used to in the days when.

He turned to the computer and brought up his email programme. It took him a while to work out what he wanted to say but he finished it eventually.

Thank you very much for the scooter and so on. I am sorry it got wrecked. I think it was a good idea of Yours to wangle the money to pay for it, though. I don't think I am very safe with it on the whole, so I won't get another one. Money is still a problem although the lorry episode has helped. I will repay the credit card company.

The manager at the supermarket needs a good talking to in my opinion, he should have told me how to deal with that artichoke thing. What is the point of artichokes?

Regards

William Penfold

Administrative Manager

In the evening, he went to the pub and shared a convivial evening with Jimmy, who was rambling on as usual about the state of the world and his wallet. William kept quiet about his changed fortunes. He needed to think about what to do. About his future. Did he have a future? There was a thought. They parted company a little on the early side and he proceeded home, more steady than was his wont.

Once home, he decided to go upstairs. He wasn't sure why he wanted to do this but the thought of kipping down on the sofa suddenly seemed rather uncomfortable. Rather undignified. He was accompanied up the stairs by Ginger and he made it to the main front bedroom. The bed looked very rumpled and forlorn, there was a thick layer of dust on the battered old dressing table and the door of the wardrobe was swinging open. Still, he decided to go through with his plan of sleeping upstairs, in a proper bed. More or less, it has to be said, because he was somewhat frightened of going back down the stairs. Nevertheless, he pulled the bedclothes together and began to undress. At that point, he realised he didn't have any pyjamas with him. Still, he didn't have any downstairs either, so that was not, after all, a problem. He curled up under the duvet and Ginger made himself comfortable on top.

CHAPTER 8

He slept well and woke up early in the morning; he was instantly alarmed, not recognising where he was for a minute. Then he went to the bathroom and discovered he had soap but no towel. He wondered where he kept the towels. Did he have towels, plural? What had he done with the one that had been there? Carefully he began the dangerous descent down the stairs, impeded in this by the efforts of Ginger, whose aim in life, like all cats, was to trip him up on the way down. Once down, he washed himself in the handbasin of the downstairs loo, where there was one reasonable towel. He made himself a cup of tea, fed the cat, and then realised he would have to upstairs again to retrieve his clothes. Damn!

Grimly, he ascended the stairs, made his bed and got dressed. He found he urgently needed a drink. A proper drink. After a precarious trip downstairs, he found his jacket on a hook in the hall, with his baseball cap, which he placed carefully on his head.

He was just opening a can of beer when the doorbell went. It was the men from Social Services. Two of them this time. One was older, a bit portly and had a moustache. The other was younger and scruffier. He vaguely remembered them from a previous visit some time ago. The scruffy one held a folder in his hand.

"Hello, William. We are your carers, from the Social Services."

He didn't remember giving them permission to call him William. He drew himself up and gave them a frosty look.

"Good morning, gentlemen," he said.

"How are you getting on, William?"

"I'm alright. I've had a bit of trouble with an artichoke. You ought to speak to that manager, you know. He has no idea about customer relations."

The men stared at him and then at each other. William opened the door wide and they followed him into the kitchen.

"Where's the table, William?"

"In the garden," said William.

"Why's that then?"

William thought for a moment. "I needed to clean the floor," he said. They all inspected the floor. It hadn't been cleaned in months.

The cat came in. William gave it some food and a little milk. The men looked puzzled.

"Is this your cat, William?"

"No," said William.

"William," said the older one "We need to know how you are managing. Are you still drinking rather a lot? Are you eating? Are you taking all your medications regularly?"

William considered. "I'm drinking what I want, because I like it. I have had some sausages and an artichoke, which wasn't a great success. And beans. And I'm not sure about the pills, not the blue ones, that is. What are they for?"

There was a brief silence. Then, "Well, you need something to help keep you on an even keel," said carer number one, the portly one. "We can get you some more this morning. Where do you keep your medication?"

They inspected the patch behind the toaster and the awful truth was revealed. It was clear that William had not been following his prescribed issue of pills. Carer number two, the scruffy one, made some more notes in his folder.

"Shall we help you get the table indoors?" asked the portly one. He opened the back door and the two men went out to bring the table back in. "What's that plank of wood doing there against that window?" said one of them.

"That's for the cat," explained William.

"I don't think that's a good idea."

"Well, I like it, and so does the cat," said William, suddenly belligerent.

"Are those new trousers?" asked one of them, noticing William's new attire.

"Yes," said William, cautiously. He wanted to avoid the subject of money. "Got them in a charity shop."

"And the jacket?"

"Yes."

"You did well."

They inspected the state of the washing and decided to pay a visit to the launderette, leaving one of them there in charge of the washing. After that, they would go to the chemist with a pre-prescribed prescription. Then they would go to the bank. Finally, they would call in at the launderette to collect the washing and then do some food shopping. The expedition was to be in the portly one's car, which would make it difficult for William to remember the route to the bank, which he particularly wanted to do.

"What I want to know is," said William, "is this house mine or yours?"

"The house is council property, Mr. Penfold. We became involved when it appeared you were unable, er, having difficulty with running your previous property and with looking after yourself satisfactorily." The carer's voice sounded neutral and rather prim.

So that was settled. He supposed they made sure he kept himself alive and on the right side of the law. They checked that he got all the benefits he was entitled to and paid what he could towards the bills. Presumably he had salvaged a few things from his previous life such as his jacket and the computer, bits of furniture and so on.

He wondered briefly where he had been before the Social Services got him, but he pushed the thought away firmly. They'd be on about the past in no time, given half a chance. What he needed to know was had he got any money of his own and could he get his hands on it? Without their knowing?

"How are you feeling, William?"

"Feeling about what?"

"Well, about managing on your own, for instance. Are you still drinking a lot?"

"What do you mean, a lot?"

He found he was still holding a just-opened can of beer as he spoke.

"Do you start drinking early in the morning, for instance?"

"Mind your own business," said William, suddenly exasperated. "I just happened to have this can handy."

"I suggest we get all the washing together," said the portly one.

"What about the stuff upstairs?" asked William. "The bed things?"

"You've been upstairs?"

"And there's my old trousers."

William was giving them surprises, he could see.

"And," he said, emphasising his words, "I wish to buy some pyjamas."

"Right, well, William, let's get going."

They got going. They stopped off at the launderette and left the scruffy one in charge of the washing, whilst William and the portly one went to the chemist. Then they were off to the bank. William tried hard to remember the roads and the name of the bank, which was a building society called the Protect and Save Society. Guided by his carer William eventually arrived at the front of the queue. He dutifully signed the form thrust at him by the portly one, who gave it, folded inside a red passbook of some description, to a bored-looking cashier.

"How much have I got?" asked William.

"Beg your pardon?" said the cashier, who had jumped slightly at William's abrupt question.

"I said how much have I got?" repeated William loudly.

"Well, you have all the benefits paid in this month, but do you have any other account?"

"I don't know, do I?" said William. "Could have a lot somewhere else, stashed away, which I don't know of. Secret nest egg they haven't told me about."

"Just a minute, William," said the portly one. "I think you do have another account, but it's your savings you know, not very much, well under the limit, if you go too high you won't get any benefits and if you take too much of it out that's it, all gone, so it's best…"

"Are you telling me I can't have my own money?" shouted William, about to launch into one of his manic rages.

"Of course you can but have you got the number of the other account, or the other passbook?" asked the cashier.

"I don't know the number," said William, "how am I supposed to remember all this? Nobody tells me anything. It's as bad as the artichoke. You tell me what I've got."

"Have your, er, friends got the passbook?" asked the cashier.

The portly one looked alarmed. "Well, yes, I expect it's in your folder. Robert's got your folder with him," he said weakly.

"Well, this is a disgrace. A disgrace," shouted William, excitedly. "All this time I've had money, I've even asked God for it, and you've kept it from me. We'll have to go back to the launderette and get it from what's-his-name."

"Just a minute," said the cashier. "I can tell you what you have in your other account. Can you prove who you are?"

"Why should I do that?" asked William, thoroughly enraged now. "I know who I am."

"Have you got your passport with you? Or a credit or debit card? Or a utility bill?"

William did have a credit card with him, but he wasn't going to let on about that. "No, I haven't. I don't take my passport round with me just to please idiots in banks."

"Please don't be abusive, Mr. Penfold, " said the cashier. "I'm sure your friend will vouch for you and you are in receipt of benefits. Do you have anything to prove Mr.Penfold's entitlement, Sir, which I can use as proof of identity?" she asked of the carer.

"Oh dear. All the paperwork is in the folder. At the launderette."

"It's a disgrace," said William. "An absolute disgrace. Probably illegal. That's my money and I can't get it. I shall," he paused, searching for something really threatening, "consult my solicitors," he finished triumphantly.

"Can you people get a move on?" said a disgruntled voice from the now extensive queue behind him.

"Let's just get you your money for now," said the portly one, pacifically, "then we'll go and get the rest of the paperwork from Robert later. This they did, with the portly one taking charge of the proceedings.

CHAPTER 9

Eventually they left the bank, William still shouting and waving his hands in the air and demanding a drink to help him cope with all these idiots, and the portly one all flustered and trying to be soothing at the same time. They made two stops on the way to the launderette, once to the chemist's to collect William's prescription medication, where he created another scene of put-upon fury, demanding to know why he had to wait so long to get his blue pills and demanding to know what they were for, then not believing the chemist, and secondly to a men's outfitter's, where he became involved in a fierce argument with the shop assistant about elasticated waists as opposed to cords which had to be tied on the pyjamas that he most liked. The portly one, who volunteered the fact that he was called Denis, had had enough by now and steered William out of the shop and to the launderette, where they collected Robert and his folder and William's laundry.

Denis took them all back to William's house before it could be suggested that they all went back to the bank. They seemed to forget about the shopping that they usually did.

They were greeted by Ginger, who had taken yet another sausage onto the rug in the living room. William, in a placatory mood now, offered to make them a cup of tea, which seemed to amaze them, and they settled down, Robert on a rather rickety chair and Denis on the sofa, to discuss how Mr. Penfold was getting on, looking at all the utilities bills they had accumulated, which they seemed to be on top of, and to reinforce the idea of him taking all his medication, at the right time. They even made him out a daily list, which they wanted to put in a prominent position somewhere near the toaster. They discussed his benefits and told him exactly when they would call again. William really wanted them to drink their tea and go; he needed to sort his money out himself and decide what to do with it, but they were still reluctant to leave without establishing a few more facts.

William could contain his impatience no longer. "Well, where's my passbook then?"

Robert fished it out of the mass of papers on his lap.

"Look," said William, excitedly, "I've got £3,465 here. It's mine. I could have had two pairs of those pyjamas," he said accusingly to Denis.

"And no doubt another artichoke," said Denis pointedly. "That isn't the question, is it? The point is..."

"The point is, it's mine. Do I get a cheque book with this?" he asked suddenly.

"Well, no doubt you could have one, but listen, William, £3,000 sounds a lot of money, but it wouldn't last long. It's all you have. It's all you have left over from – "

"From the days when," said William.

"Yes, well, it wouldn't keep you going for long, would it?

Do you think you might be better off in a Home, and not having to bother with all this?"

William stared at him, open-mouthed.

"I mean, you are obviously doing so much better with the drinking so you might find you get on better with people now…" but even as he spoke memories of the scenes in the bank, the chemist's and the gent's outfitter's reminded Denis that this was not true.

"You want to put me in a Home?" roared William. "In a Home?" His face turned purple, which frightened the two carers somewhat. He looked round for a weapon but all he could find was his new long umbrella, which he picked up and waved in a wild manner.

"Get out of my house this minute," he said, "and don't come back ever again. Until I need a new prescription," he added hastily, thinking of that and all those bills he might have to deal with once they had washed their hands of him. "I'm alright here and so's the cat. Go away, go on, go away." He shooed them out of the sitting room.

The two men retreated hastily to Denis' car, where they sat for a long time, talking and filling in forms from Robert's folder. Had William 'got religion'? Denis remembered his reference to God. And there was the curious mention of artichokes. That did not fit in with any known personality disorder that they could identify. William glared at them from the front room window, waving his umbrella.

Then he sat down and started to consider the position. How much money did he have and what was the best way to spend it?

He thought for a moment of why he had told God that

not having money was his principal problem, because he didn't have enough to spend on drink. He wasn't absolutely sure that that was absolutely true any more. However, the thought of drink sidetracked him somewhat and he went to the kitchen to find something to slake his thirst. The cat also came and began to demand attention. He fed it and gave it some milk, after which it went out for a breath of fresh air and William began to prepare a meal for himself.

After some bacon, eggs, sausage and fried bread, with a can of lager, he felt very much better, less angry, more self-satisfied. A Home indeed! I expect they helped me a lot just after the time when, he thought. But I'm better now. I can manage. Well, most things. Not the paperwork things perhaps. Which reminded him about the money. He had decisions to make.

How much did he owe to the credit card company? How much actual cash did he have at his disposal? He'd told God he was going to pay off the debt but it would still leave a lot which he could do what he liked with.

Firstly he looked again at the credit card company's letter. It told him he owed £4,097 or a minimum of £125; there was an envelope with in which he could post his payment. He then looked in his pockets for the remains of the £75 he had started out with some time ago. There were very few remains; he had £12.27 left. He then studied the large brown envelope which contained the lorry driver's £5,000, which, he now realised, Denis had been sitting on all afternoon. Lastly, he looked at his passbook from the Protect and Save Society. He had £3,465 in there. It was both satisfying and worrying, satisfying because he could buy a few things and not have to be too bothered about the cost but worrying because he knew, somehow, that it would all eventually disappear and there was no discernible way of increasing it.

Then of course there was the money that the Social Services had left him to live on. They had totted up what he would have to pay for the electric, the gas, the water, the rates, the rent and all that stuff and left him with £300. That was for food and drink, haircuts, clothes and so on. When would they turn up again? This time they had said…what? He couldn't remember. He remembered that they had left in a hurry, because he had thrown them out. Why did he do that? Thinking back, it was something to do with something they had said, but it had all gone now. Stupid fools, bothering a respectable, law-abiding citizen like him. Were they coming back in a month's time? Or two weeks? No, it was no use, it had gone.

All this money business was a great worry. Well, how much should he give the credit card company? On balance he decided to pay it all off, seeing as how he had got his own source now. Then he wouldn't be afraid of someone finding out about the scooter. He'd still have the card and he could buy things from time to time. God would be pleased.

The thought of God reminded him about his electronic communications. Warily, he eyed the computer. There was, he discovered, an email in his inbox. Cautiously, he opened it. There was an email from God. It said:

There is more to life than artichokes. Try to do more.

As usual, William flew into a rage. What use was this sort

of advice! Do more what? A cookery course? What sort of life was He talking about? He was already feeding a cat for Christ's sake. That was quite enough to cope with. He'd been involved in a terrible accident and nearly mown down by an errant white van driver. And he was persecuted by these Social Service men who wanted to put him in a Home! The memory came flooding back at this point. They also kept on trying to get him talking about the Past, which he was not going to do. The Past was obviously dreadful and he had no intention of raking it all up, just to please them, interfering so-and-so's.

He got up and stormed towards the kitchen, in a tottery sort of way, flailing his arms about as he went. There he found a couple of cans of lager and the cat, who appeared to be hungry and thirsty again. Grumbling to himself, he fed it and gave it some milk, then went back to the sitting room, where he hunted around for the credit card letter. Eventually, he found it. It had an empty reply letter inside it, into which he started to put £4,000 from the big brown envelope from the lorry driver but then he remembered it would be better if he could send all the correct money by cheque, if he could get a cheque book from the Protect and Save branch. All he had to do was remember where the branch was.

He laid down on the sofa and tried very hard to remember which way he had gone in the car. He thought he could remember the way to the launderette and the chemist. It was the bit beyond that that confused him. Hang on! If he could look up the address in the phone book or Yellow Pages, it would be a simple matter of just asking someone, wouldn't it? But then, he hadn't got a phone book. He didn't have a phone. The Social Services didn't seem to think he could manage one.

Stupid interfering fools. He felt the anger rising up in him. He'd have to go, but go where?

The library! That's where he would go. He knew where that was. He'd been thrown out of it only a few weeks ago! For making a disturbance. He couldn't remember what it had been about but the reaction of the staff had been quite disgraceful, he did remember that. And he did know where the library was.

"Right, I'm off." He picked up his cap and umbrella and buttoned up his jacket. He left the cat sleeping peacefully on the rug.

"Bye," he said, "shan't be long."

CHAPTER 10

Two streets away William entered the local library. It was an old-fashioned and rather dingy building. As he went in, he came to a large area lined with computers and rows of DVDs and CDs.

He stared around him. "What have you done with all the books, then?" he inquired of a lady behind a polished desk.

"What book do you require, Sir?" she said, helpfully.

"I need to know where something is," he said.

"Well, all the books are in order of subject matter," she began, helpfully. "There's Crime, over there, behind the DVDs, and then Romance, then –"

"I don't want Romance," said William. "That's rubbish. I want –" here he paused. What did he want? He thought hard. "I want Banks. Where they are, I mean."

"Well, there is a financial section upstairs, Sir. You'll find everything you need to know about Barclays and Lloyds and so on up there."

"I don't want Barclays. Where's the lift?"

"I'm afraid there isn't one. The stairs are at the far end."

"Are you telling me there's no lift? How am I supposed to manage? I've got a dodgy knee."

As usual, anger welled up inside him. He was about to launch into one of his tirades against the injustice of this world in not providing lifts for him when he needed one when a gentleman appeared who was welcomed by the library assistant as 'our Mr.Fairweather who will be able to assist you, he knows a lot about banks,' after which she disappeared with relief.

Mr. Fairweather, who did indeed know a lot about banks, was able to point William in the right direction. The bank was a building society called the Protect and Save and it was situated on the High Street. Mr. Fairweather gave him detailed instructions, then explained that the No. 74 bus would take him straight there.

On the way out, he came across a desk where they issued, or at least allowed you to apply for, bus passes. He had not got one.Why hadn't he got one? Those Social men should have got him one. They had failed in their duty of care again! He could catch this No. 74 and go straight there! That library man had said so. He became very angry. By the time he had got to the desk and was engaging with the hapless young woman who staffed it he was already furious.

"How can I help you, Sir?" inquired the assistant brightly with a beaming smile.

"Why haven't I got a bus pass?" he shouted, waving his umbrella.

"Well, when did you apply for one?"

"I didn't. I think I should just have got one, not have to go through all this rigmarole."

"Well, all I want is your address and a few personal details. Have you got proof of identification, a debit or credit card perhaps?"

That set him off again. "It's as bad as the bank. I know who I am. I just want a bus pass so that I can get to the bank. To get a debit card," he added. "Then I can prove who I am." That'll floor her, he thought. But she continued with her list of questions.

She persevered. "What is your date of birth?"

That was difficult. He had no idea. "May 11th," he said, "1912."

She looked at him suspiciously. "You don't look that old."

"Are you going to give me my bus pass or not?" He waved his umbrella menacingly. The girl looked round in desperation. She was saved by the arrival of Mr. Fairweather and another senior assistant. The senior assistant unfortunately remembered William from his previous visit to the library. Shortly after William found himself outside the building again, having been escorted by the two men, despite his noisy protests.

"I shall take the matter further," he shouted, as they turned to go back inside.

"You do that, Mr. Penfold," replied the senior assistant. And that was that.

"Prats," muttered William. The whole world was against him. He marched up the street and endeavoured to remember the instructions from Mr. Fairweather. Rather surprisingly, he did find the High Street and, eventually, the Protect and Save Building Society.

It was closed.

William felt he had never been so angry. Here he was, a

man of substance, with £4,000 in his wallet (suddenly he remembered it wasn't! He hadn't brought the lorry driver's money with him!) and a further £3,000 in an account and he couldn't get inside to demand a cheque book. Perhaps it was for the best. But still they ought to be open. How could people like himself conduct their substantial and important financial affairs when they were not given their bus passes and were then messed about by tinpot bureaucrats like people who worked in banks?

He set off home, longing for a drink and for someone to let off steam to. He paused on the way home to buy a few food and drink essentials, cornflakes, a large pork pie, bottles of beer and so on with some of the £300 from the Social Services men, which he discovered he had with him. When he got home he was greeted enthusiastically by the cat and settled down to have a calming drink. What a day! He pondered his options. He had no idea when the Protect and Save would be open again. Maybe tomorrow. Maybe they'd gone on holiday. Who knows? He thought of the credit card company. He had to pay that money. He'd told God he would pay them. It was a Debt of Honour.

He found the envelope they had sent him. He needed to send them £4,097. Slowly, he began to put 82 £50 notes into the envelope. It was no use. It just wasn't big enough. Once more he had been defeated by organisational incompetence. Grumbling and muttering, he thought what to do. He looked again at the large brown envelope in which the money had originally been given to him by the lorry driver. There was still money in there of course. There was no name or address on it. He could use that. So slowly, carefully, he began to sort it all out, putting 82 £50 notes into the large brown envelope. When he had done that he remembered that the credit card company had demanded £4090. There had been a sizeable fee for delivery, on top of the bill for his umbrella and so on. He looked at the money he had been left by the Social men and also whatever money he had left of his own, plus the £1,000 left over from the lorry driver. He could only assemble £4,100 but it would have to do. Feeling rather grand and rich he inserted the paperwork from the credit card company and signed it, writing 'Keep the Change' in big letters across the form. He signed all the bits that appeared to need a signature. He sealed the envelope, relieved at having done his duty.

At that point, he realised he had put the piece of paper with the credit card address on it inside the brown envelope. Anger welled up again but there was absolutely no-one he could blame for the incident but himself. He calmed down with relief when he found he still had the empty envelope from the credit card company. Carefully, he copied the address. He wondered if one first class stamp would cover it. Probably not, he thought, they get you for everything these days. All he had to do now was buy the stamps tomorrow and send it off.

He did wonder if they would be annoyed at getting their money in cash but the thought did not really trouble him. People were glad enough to get any money back, he reckoned; they weren't going to say no. They should consider themselves lucky to have got it at all. With that thought still uppermost in his mind, he went to the kitchen to make himself a meal. Ginger came with him.

He had another fry up of sorts, which was quite filling and

satisfactory, and fed the cat, who seemed to like cooked sausage as much as raw. Remembering the laundry he wondered if any of it would have to be ironed. The bed linen could go straight onto the bed, no question. T-shirts – no, underwear – no – trousers? His old blue trousers that he had been wearing before the arrival of the cream, red-striped ones? Yes, perhaps they could do with a bit of smartening up, he reckoned. But that was all. He gathered up the sheets, pillow cases and, with what turned out to be a duvet cover, he set off upstairs. There he discovered the irritating difficulty inherent in putting a duvet cover onto a duvet; in the end he completely lost his temper and just laid the cover on top of it. 'That'll have to do,' he told Ginger, who had come upstairs with him. But the room looked a little fresher and cleaner for his efforts. He wandered into the other bedroom, which didn't contain anything much, just a few bits and pieces of furniture and a large rug. He looked out of the window. He looked down at his garden, which seemed to consist of unidentifiable rubbish, with an old, broken-down shed at the bottom, next to the gate which led out to the alley beyond.

"Garden's a disgrace, Ginger," he said. "P'raps I'll try to clear it up a bit."

He looked at Mrs. Brenner's garden. That *was* a garden, a proper garden, with flowers and things. Already it was beginning to look a bit overgrown. The grass needed mowing, bushes needed cutting back, the hedge needed clipping. He remembered God's instructions – TLC for Mrs. B. and he, William, had to start to 'do something more'. It wasn't something he would have chosen to do, he knew. What did he know about gardening? Anyway, he hadn't got any gardening tools. But wait, there might be something in the near-derelict tumbledown old shed at the bottom of his own garden. He didn't think that he'd ever been in it, actually. There could be something left by the previous tenant. He'd have a look tomorrow.

With that thought he turned, went downstairs carefully, because of the cat, and set off for the pub.

The pub was not a success that night. They were holding a quiz and he and Jimmy hadn't got a team and no-one seemed to want them to help make up theirs. They shouted out whatever they thought was the correct answer whenever they could but it never was and they gave up after a while. 'Quizzes,' said Jimmy, "get in the way of intelligent conversation.'

"Yes," said William, mournfully. "They're not interested in the right answers, anyway."

"No," said Jimmy. "They just make 'em up."

As he made his unsteady way home that night, he began to be beset by unwanted thoughts. Why had he been thrown out of so many places? Twice he had been ejected from the big supermarket, once when he was, wrongfully and embarrassingly, accused of shoplifting and once again, when he was on his mobility scooter and had actual money to pay for things. Twice he had been thrown out of the library, the last time just for asking for a bus pass. He couldn't remember what the problem was the first time. He'd thrown the social workers out of his house at least once. Wherever he went there were always rows. Why were there always rows? Why didn't he have friends, other than Jimmy Donovan? And he didn't count him as a friend, you couldn't talk to Jimmy Donovan. The man was basically an idiot. He was just there as a drinking mate. He did remember Mrs. Brenner's reference to 'my friend Mr. Penfold' though and that cheered him up a little.

When he let himself in Ginger met him in the hallway and began to demand food and fuss. "Well, it's you and me against the world I guess, Ginger," he said. He fed the animal and took a couple of bottles of beer back to the sitting room, with some cheese biscuits he'd forgotten he'd bought. He sat on the sofa in a cloud of grumpy self-pity.

"Do I drink too much because I'm miserable, Ginger, or am I miserable because I drink too much?"

The cat did not express an opinion but went to sleep next to him. Usually anger welled up inside of him, anger at everything that gone wrong, that had landed him in this kind of purposeless life, anger at everything and everybody, but tonight the fires were muted, stilled. He was afraid. Did that mean that the demons were coming, that depression was slowly creeping up on him, ready to bring him down? Was he due for another spell in the place with the red curtains? What had they done there? Had they been trying to get him to drink less? Or was it a place where you learned to stop being so angry and recall the past? He opened another bottle whilst he considered this.

After five minutes' earnest consideration, he said, "Load of nonsense. Well, bedtime, Ginger, where are you going to sleep?" The cat elected to go with him to the foot of the stairs and, very unsteadily in William's case, they both climbed to the top and went into the reasonable tidy front bedroom, with the clean duvet cover spread out and William's new pyjamas neatly folded on the pillow.

"Tell you what, Ginger. I'll see if there's anything to be

done about Mrs. B.'s garden tomorrow. Or mine. And we'll buy a few more things and see if we can get a bus pass as well. After all, we have got £1,000 in ready cash, £300 from the Social men and over £3,000 in the bank, even if I can't get at it. What do you think of that then?"

The cat ignored his comments, jumped on the bed and curled up ready for sleep, whilst William pondered the problems involved in having disposable income. He didn't want to spend it all on drink. Or on food. What was it God had said? 'There's more to life than artichokes.' Very profound. God had told him to 'Do More'. That non-specific directive had made him angry at first, but, come to think of it, although he could still feel a certain nagging anger that the bank had been shut, maybe it was something to do with their opening hours, he suddenly thought. He'd get a cheque book somehow. It was his human right. And he would 'do more'. With that he too fell asleep.

CHAPTER 11

The next day dawned sunny and bright. William woke up, for once eager to get up and get on with it. He wasn't sure what 'it' was, but he knew he wanted to do something. He had a shower, got dressed and had fed the cat all before 9 o'clock, which was unprecedented for him. Breakfast was coffee, cornflakes, toast and the proper number and kind of pills as prescribed by the Social men, in their instructions left behind the toaster. Pleased with himself for this foray into normal living, he opened a bottle of beer and took it into the garden.

He approached the tumbledown shed at the bottom of his garden with some trepidation, suspecting that all he would find would be dirt and spiders. Dirt and spiders there were in abundance, but there was also an old-fashioned lawnmower, covered with a protective sheeting, a spade, a garden fork and a pair of rather rusty old shears, together with an assortment of gardening equipment, bundles of string, gardening gloves, baskets, plastic bins, bags and various bottles and packages containing stuff to make things grow and stuff to kill off things that are already growing.

"Bingo, Ginger," he said. Ginger was interested in the shed and emerged from beneath a pile of old rags covered in a layer of cobwebs and unidentifiable mess that changed him from a ginger to a tabby feline!

With some difficulty, William managed to pull the lawnmower out of the shed, covering himself in hanging cobwebs as he did so, and out into the open space of his garden, where he could inspect it properly. It was an ancient one of a very simple design and there didn't seem to be anything obviously wrong with it. He could not, however, try it out on his own garden, there being little grass of any description there, only dirt and stones and rubbish, interspersed with the occasional struggling patch of green.

The next problem then presented itself. How could he get into Mrs. Brenner's property, together with the riches of his shed, in order to carry out his plan of garden maintenance? He pushed the lawnmower up to the dividing hedge, which was rather wild and unkempt on his side, and viewed the situation. He tried to lift the mower, but it was far too heavy for him, the hedge was far too high and he had to admit defeat. He felt a little shoot of anger growing inside him but before it could turn into one of his rages he saw a possible solution. Mrs. Brenner, like himself, had a door at the bottom of her garden which opened on to the alley. Quickly, he went through his own door, into the alleyway, and pushed on her door. It was locked!

Furious and disappointed he returned to his own area, and felt the need for a drink coming upon him. Still angry and muttering to himself, he turned to go into his kitchen to fetch another beer, if there was one. Coming out, bottle in hand, he looked across the hedge which divided her property from his. He had a good vantage point from where he was standing as the hedge was a little lower near the kitchen; there was even a bit of a gap through which he could look straight down over her lawn. He looked long and hard down her garden at the alleyway door. There seemed to be no sign of a padlock on it. Could he just make out a couple of bolts? He could. He was sure he could. So all he had to do was hop over the hedge himself and undo the bolts, then wheel the lawnmower in. Problem solved!

To 'hop over the hedge', as he put it to himself, was not the easiest thing in the world for a man of his age (whatever that was) and in his condition. With the aid of a chair from the kitchen, on which he climbed rather perilously, and by dint of hanging onto the branch of a small tree in his neighbour's hedge, which unfortunately split in two as it took his weight, he did manage to propel himself into the desired area, although he did arrive flat on his back, bedecked with branches and bits of greenery, with his feet in the air. Scrambling, with difficulty, to his feet, he went straight to the door and found, to his delight, that indeed it was secured by two bolts, top and bottom. These he undid, went round to his own home and duly wheeled in the lawnmower. Now for the real business of tidying up Mrs. Brenner's garden. God had said 'Do More' and he was going to Do More.

First he needed that drink, which he had left on the ground near his kitchen. He could see that gardening was going to be hard work, so he brought yet another bottle of beer from the kitchen with him. On the way back, he picked up several bits, useful things, from his shed. He didn't think he would need a spade, but he took the shears and a plastic bin to put rubbish in, also a contraption to fix on to the front of the lawnmower to catch the grass cuttings. All these things he put in the plastic bin. Thus equipped, he sat down on Mrs. Brenner's lawn, emptied the bin and studied the situation. The beer was most refreshing. Eventually, he stirred himself and began to mow the lawn.

It was not a big lawn and he began mowing from the kitchen end down to the alleyway door end and back. The lines were a little wobbly, it was true, especially where he came up against the pile of things he had taken from his shed, the bin, the shears and, he realised, the grass cuttings container. He paused to fix this on to the lawnmower, which he did after something of a struggle. He continued mowing a little erratically for a while before feeling that he needed a bit of a rest. He was aching and a little sore from where he had tumbled over the hedge. It was a hot day and he had, it is true, exerted himself rather more than usual. He sat down on the grass and opened the second bottle of beer. Ginger, still covered in cobwebs, joined him, carrying something that he had filched from the kitchen, possibly half a pork pie. Filled with a sense of having done something 'More', as God had suggested, something worthwhile, William, also bestrewn with cobwebs and with foliage from his adventurous arrival into the garden, dozed off and Ginger curled up beside him.

Two doors down, a neighbour, Maisie Watson, looking out of her back bedroom window, saw what she thought was a dirty old drunk, covered in cobwebs and complete with two beer bottles, lying, presumably drunk and insensible, in the middle of Mrs. Brenner's lawn. She didn't see the lawnmower as it was shielded from her vision by the hedges in between. She knew Mrs. Brenner was in hospital. Naturally she did what every law-abiding citizen should do in such circumstances. She phoned the police.

It took the rest of the day to sort it all out. A Panda car with two constables, rather young and very keen, arrived outside Mrs. Brenner's and they had almost taken the decision to break down the door, fearing for her safety, before the neighbour who had phoned spotted them (she was a keen member of Neighbourhood Watch) and guided them to the alleyway at the back. Here they had a prolonged interview with William, whom they initially suspected of stealing the lawnmower and other articles from Mrs. Brenner. They took him down to the police station, in the Panda car, where the station sergeant was unfortunately out, attending a course on Good Police Relations with the General Public, and a great argument broke out.

William said it was his lawnmower but the police thought this was unlikely, as he didn't have a lawn. They accused him of breaking and entering into his neighbour's property, but he explained he was driven by altruistic motives of wanting to do some garden maintenance next door. This struck them as also very unlikely. They then accused him of being drunk in charge of a vehicle. He said it wasn't petrol driven so it wasn't a vehicle and he wasn't drunk anyway. They then breathalysed him, which proved he had been drinking but not that he was especially drunk.

One of the men recognised him as having caused some disturbance in the big supermarket a few months ago. William, who was by now consumed with rage, made matters worse by shouting and swearing, somewhat incomprehensibly, about God, emails, artichokes, mobility scooters, white van drivers and especially the police. Things began to look bad and William demanded to see his solicitor. They asked who his solicitor was and of course he did not have the least idea. They sent for the duty solicitor, who happened to be in the station at the time, who attended, rather less than enthusiastic at being involved with the misbehaviour of an elderly drunk.

By this time the station had had enough of William. The older, more experienced station sergeant had come back from his course, the younger, very keen policemen who had brought William in had been cut down to size and Mrs. Watson, the neighbour who had reported him, had turned up and now recognised him as the man who lived next door to Mrs. Brenner. She had phoned the Social Services, knowing that William had regular visits from them, and now Denis and Robert had also arrived. All William's anger was still going strong. He was blazing away at everybody, especially at the neighbour who had called the police, and announced his intention of suing everybody who was intent on making his life a misery, including the Social Services, who had not provided him with a bus pass.

Eventually he was released and Denis and Robert took him home in Denis' car. They told the police they would see to the mess in Mrs. Brenner's garden and look after William. They sympathised with him, expressed their astonishment at his efforts with Mrs. Brenner's garden and his foray into the old shed. They made him a cup of tea and fixed up a light meal and were altogether of much more use than they usually were. They fed Ginger. Mrs. Watson came round to apologise to William, with a friend from No. 63, Mrs. Jenkins, who was very curious about the whole incident, and they also had a cup of tea. William began to feel that he was supported by a small circle of friends, a very unusual feeling for him. There is of course nothing like being unfairly treated by the police to ensure that one has a respected standing in the community.

Denis and Robert retrieved the lawnmower and gardening objects from Mrs. Brenner's and put them back in William's shed, which they tried to make waterproof. There only remained the problem of how to fasten the back door to the alleyway from Mrs Brenner's garden. Eventually, Robert was prevailed upon to enter by the same means that William had, although returning by that route was very much more difficult. As he was scruffy to start with the damage to his appearance was less bothersome than it would have been had Denis undertaken the task. Mrs. Brenner's lawn had undoubtedly taken a beating and was left in a troubled and trampled state. Her hedge had also been somewhat damaged. The Social Service men were comforting. "It will repair itself, you'll see," they said.

William raised the issue of the bus pass. Apparently they had actually provided him with one, some time ago. It was likely that William had torn it up in a temper or otherwise lost it, unfortunately. They agreed to get him a new one.

When William arrived at the pub that evening he was amazed to discover that the events of the day were now common knowledge and had become somewhat embroidered and glorified in the telling. He had changed from being Community Nuisance to Local Hero, with a tendency to take a little drink now and then but with a Heart of Gold, a man who looked after his neighbour's cat while its owner was in hospital and even tried to look after her garden, a man who had been persecuted and fitted up by the Old Bill and nearly put in prison for being a decent neighbour. Numerous people offered to buy him a drink and a lady with a large shopping bag gave him a tin of cat food for Ginger. It was all very gratifying and he thoroughly enjoyed himself.

That night he slept well.

Chapter 12

Next day dawned bright and sunny again. He had a little bit of a hangover and it took him some time to work out why, as he had usually had a few drinks the night before and rarely felt any ill effects. Ah yes – the pub! The atmosphere, the congratulations, the handshakes! He remembered it all distinctly, though he couldn't quite fix on why that was. Something to do with the police, he thought. Gradually it all came back. The gardening episode at Mrs. Brenner's, the police and their absurd accusations, the uproar in the police station, the lawyer, the neighbour, the Social Services chaps, the ride home, the vindication of his total innocence, the resultant congratulations – he savoured the memories at the same time as he decided, despite the hangover, to cook a proper breakfast. "Come on, Ginger," he said to a still sleeping cat, "up you get. We've got a lot to do."

He looked round the room. "Why haven't I got a dressing gown?" he inquired of nobody in particular. "I shall buy one today," he announced. He and Ginger descended the stairs carefully and he then began to search the kitchen for anything that might make up a decent breakfast. He found some bacon, eggs, sausages, bread, cornflakes, tea and some pork pie which looked as though it needed eating up. He fed Ginger first with a tin of cat food he found lying on the table (he had no idea where it had come from) and followed it up with some milk. Then, with some gusto, he began to cook himself the best breakfast he had had in months.

Afterwards, he had a good shower and took care with his shaving and dressing. At that point he suddenly thought of his computer. Surely he should fill God in with all that had happened? Well, of course, He would already know, being God and a super know-all, but all the same he felt he should at least tell Him what had happened when he had tried to Do More, as He had advised him. It hadn't gone how he'd planned, but nevertheless it had all turned out alright, as it happened. So he sat down at his computer and called up his emails.

Dear God

I did try to Do More, like you suggested, but Mrs. Brenner's garden proved to be a bit difficult, due to that Mrs. Watson making a big mistake and the police being quite disgraceful. I would report them, only I don't know who to report them to. Do you think the Home Secretary is the right person to deal with it?

I am beginning to feel much more myself now, thank you very much for your help, although I can't remember anything about why I'm living here, or where I used to live before. Do you think it matters? I would go and visit Mrs. Brenner again only I haven't got the scooter thing and I haven't got a bus pass yet so don't go on about her needing TLC because the journey is impossible with Ginger. I think the garden is probably a bit beyond me.

Have you got any more good suggestions?
I am paying all my debts to the Credit Card Company.
Yours sincerely
William Penfold
Administrative Manager

He studied this for some time before deciding it was suitable. Eventually he pressed Send and set off for the shops, taking the large envelope addressed to the credit card company with him, which he had found inexplicably lying behind the toaster, with the Social people's instructions, when he was looking for his pills.

His visit to the post office provoked a bit of a scene as he was unaware that large envelopes now cost more, according to size, than small ones, and his protests at the injustice of it met with no response. But as he was unlikely to be sending any more large envelopes he eventually ceased shouting about it. He paid up and continued on his way to the mini-market. There he stocked up with various basics, some impulse buys and as much beer and lager as he could carry. Fortunately there were no artichokes. He tried to remember where the dressing gown shop was but his mental map of the streets became fuzzy so he gave up and went home. He bought himself a newspaper to bone up on the Prime Minister, as he put it to himself.

Once home, he poured himself a lager, fed the cat and they both settled down on the sofa to consider matters. He felt a little different, he thought. More in control – that was it. More solid. Less – what was the word? Less excitable. Less likely to launch into one of his furious tirades. Certainly the world was quite mad, these days, not like the days when, but there was nothing he could do about it. You couldn't put it all right, could you? Perhaps it was actually something to do with the days when. Perhaps the Social people were right. Perhaps it would be better for him to remember things as they were in the days when, then he would know, somehow, when it was alright for him to lose his temper in these new days that he didn't understand and when it was not a good thing to do. Thinking about this was complicated and he began to feel a bit tired. At the back of it all was another question. Where did God come into it? What about the emails?

His train of thought was interrupted by a ring on the doorbell. It was Mrs. Watson! The one who had reported him to the police but who had then come round to apologise yesterday. Still feeling guilty and thinking that she had lost some standing in the eyes of her neighbours, she obviously wanted to make amends. Her method of making amends consisted of bringing round an apple pie and a small pot of cream. William was enormously impressed. No-one, as far as he knew, had ever given him an apple pie before. Life was certainly looking up. He didn't quite know what to do, what the etiquette was when receiving an apple pie from a hitherto largely unknown neighbour, but in the end he invited her in for a cup of coffee.

Mrs. Watson settled down on William's sofa, stroked Ginger and started to chat. "Your name's William, isn't it? Mine's Maisie. You live on your own, William?"

"Yes."

"You ever been married?"

No question she might have asked could be more awkward than that one. Had he been married? He had no idea. What on earth could he say? It was embarrassing. Desperately he looked at the ceiling but the answer was not written up there. In the end he said, in a rather strangled voice, "I don't like to talk about it."

But in Maisie Watson's ears no answer could have been more satisfying. It was now obvious that William was a Mystery Man, with a Romantic Past. That was why he was drinking and being miserable. He had been Hurt Badly by some unspecified woman. As William had said he didn't like to talk about it Maisie Watson was left with the enjoyable business of filling in the unknown parts of his life and her imagination was richly satisfying. She couldn't wait to call on Freda Jenkins to impart her 'ideas' which, in her eyes, had become 'news'.

Before she left, she invited William to attend the line dancing class at the Community Institute, next door to the library, which she said would bring him out of himself and do him a world of good. William doubted this very much as he had no idea what line dancing was and as far as dancing was concerned, he knew very well somehow that he couldn't do the foxtrot and it would be wise not to try. However, Maisie left him a booklet about the classes, which she 'just happened to have in her handbag', and went on her way, well pleased with the morning's efforts. William obviously needed someone to look after him and tidy him up a little. TLC – that was all. Then he would be alright. End of, as her grandson would say. She had only got to work out which one of her circle of female friends would be the one to work the miracle.

After Maisie had gone William continued his searching thoughts, which required a drink to see him through. Why had Maisie's question thrown him? He'd given the best answer he could, in the circumstances, nevertheless, the whole subject bothered him. Had he been married? What were his relationships with women like? Could he remember having sex? Did he find women irritating? Or interesting? Normally, when faced with puzzling thoughts, he would shrug it all off. If he couldn't solve it, well, forget it. Not worth getting himself into a stew about it. But, just for a moment, he wondered. He supposed the Social people knew his history. They often asked him about the past, invited him to talk about it, He always brushed them off, refused the invitation. Yet they must know something of his history. How much did they know and would they tell him if he asked?

Eventually, after going round in circles for several minutes, he said, "Bloody great mystery, Ginger. I think I'm best off without all that 'once upon a time' stuff, don't you? What's it matter what happened in the days when? Who cares? I'm doing alright at the moment. Got money in my pocket, got money in the bank. Got somewhere to live and people who bring me apple pies. Even got God on my side. Can't be bad."

He decided to make a list. He found a pen down the side of the sofa. It had probably belonged to Denis. Then he looked for a piece of paper. Eventually he made his list on the back of the Social people's instructions; it seemed to be the only piece of paper he had.

The list was as follows:

Make sure the Socials give me my bus pass
Get a cheque book
Buy a dressing gown

Think about what to do with the money
Look at the booklet that the apple pie woman gave me.
The garden
What about a telephone?

He studied this at length. Really, the first three were dependent on the return of Denis and Robert. They knew where everything was. They wouldn't be coming back for a while though. He couldn't remember exactly when they had last been with him but it wasn't so far back so it would be a week or two before they turned up again. Still he could wait a while yet, though it would be nice to have a bus pass, he thought, a little wistfully.

Now for the money. He had the best part of £1,000 in cash. And £3,000 plus in the bank. And what was left of the £300 the Social people had left him with. What was he going to do with all that?

He thought perhaps he would keep the money that was in the bank and try not to touch it, which was, after all, the advice of Denis and Robert, but he would spend the rest of it however he liked. It might lead to some difficulties in explaining his new-found affluence away but tough. He'd think of something. He felt invigorated at the thought of making decisions.

Idly, he picked up the booklet the apple pie woman had left lying on the table and studied the possibilities. You could do all sorts at the Community Institute, he discovered. Bird-watching. China painting. Bridge. Cooking for beginners. Advanced cookery. Scrabble. Art history. Life drawing. Pottery. Sculpture in stone. French. Italian. There were so many things people seemed to want to do. "Absolute rubbish, most of 'em," he told Ginger. You even had to pay to do these ridiculous things! Line dancing for instance. The apple pie woman had wanted him to go to that. But that was not his thing. Definitely not.

"I'll have to think about these classes," he told Ginger. "Most of them are in the evening. I'm not sure if it's worth missing the pub."

He looked at the rest of his list. The garden! It was a rubbish-strewn mess out there. He really couldn't manage gardens. He realised that after his abortive attempt to manage Mrs. Brenner's. Couldn't he get it paved over or something? There were several adverts in the booklet, one of which was about providing patios and paving for modern gardens. You had to phone them up and ask for a quotation. That's what he would do. He'd have it all paved over. Flattened. Tidied up. He'd get in touch with Perfect Patios tomorrow.

Brilliant! The last thing on his list was a telephone. Everyone seemed to have a mobile phone these days. Why didn't he have one? If he had one, he could get an estimate from this paving firm.

"You see what you can achieve with a bit of careful thought, Ginger," he observed. "Now let's go and fix something to eat."

The next few days passed peacefully enough, if you discount a letter of severely-worded admonition from William's credit card company. The idea of sending over £4000 in the post in cash had apparently caused uproar and great concern in their offices and, should he ever feel tempted to do any such thing again, they would withdraw his card. It was entirely reprehensible behaviour on the part of Mr. Penfold and his final flourish of 'Keep the Change' was not viewed as humorous or acceptable and they had added that amount towards his next payment. His actions had been dangerous and risked losing his money to opportunistic thieves and the company was appalled and would not be held liable for any loss if Mr. Penfold did anything so outrageously foolish again.

"Well they accepted the money, Ginger," said William, "told you they would. Pompous sods. They should be glad they got anything at all."

William concentrated on home improvements. He found an old radio at the back of a drawer in the old chest of drawers in his bedroom. He bought some batteries for it and put it in the kitchen. He bought some teacups and mugs, in case the apple pie woman came again and maybe brought her friends and hopefully some more pies, also some plates and – this was a great step forward, he bought a sugar bowl. He also began to tidy up the conglomeration of cans and bottles which lurked everywhere, not only in the kitchen. He found three underneath the sofa, which he put carefully in the dustbin. He bought another baseball cap, this time in red. There was a bath mat for the bathroom and a new, very large towel.

He also picked up a newspaper as he felt that he should be more up to date with the news. Somewhere it might say in it who the Prime Minister was. Then the Social people couldn't trip him up any more. The various items of news astonished him. He had no idea things out there were so bad and some of the things people got up to were shocking. Some of the scandals were amazing and he found them very absorbing. The Prime Minister didn't seem to be mixed up in them so he didn't find out what his name was. He'd have to use the

Internet if he really wanted to know. How had he let himself get so out of touch?

His next enterprise concerned the question of a mobile phone. He didn't really know where to get one of these. Then he remembered that the big supermarket, where he had bought his new towel, stocked them. What sort did he want? He knew there were lots of different sorts and people had a lot of trouble with them. You were always being told to turn them off. Well, he wasn't going to go to the trouble of buying one only to be told to turn it off. He needed one in order to phone the paving people. So his would be on all the time if he wanted it to be. He could feel the anger rising up inside him already at the threatened interference into his freedom to phone people.

It was still troubling him by the time he went to the pub. Jimmy Donovan wasn't there, as it happened, but William was a known face in the pub now, since his run-in with the Old Bill, and total strangers offered to buy him a drink. When he started to explain his problem about what sort of mobile he needed to buy he was overwhelmed with advice. He was steered towards buying a pay-as-you-go model and the name was written down for him so that he wouldn't have too much unwanted interference from the supermarket manager. William explained his dislike of the manager and was cheered up to discover that several of the pub's customers also disliked him and had had arguments with him. "You get what you want, William, he's well out of order, you tell him where he can put his artichokes." William felt encouraged.

CHAPTER 13

All his problems seemed to be well on the way to being resolved, once the Social people came. True, it rained the next day, but that was of no worry to someone with a large golfing umbrella and he set off towards the supermarket almost cheerfully. It wasn't a state of mind he was used to and it left him a little uneasy. Once there, he found the stand where the mobile phones were and chose the one that had been recommended to him the night before. To his relief, there was no sign of the manager and the cashier obligingly inserted the card necessary to start it all up and he brought it triumphantly home.

He also brought home a warm cooked chicken and he and Ginger shared it enthusiastically in the front room whilst watching *Prime Minister's Questions*. "So it's him, is it?" muttered William. "Who'da thought it? No good, any of 'em, Ginger. Couldn't run a whelk stall in a brewery."

His last muttered pronouncement surprised even himself and he paused to try to work out what was wrong with it before continuing with another piece of chicken. However, his use of mixed metaphors continued to baffle him so he decided to get on with sorting out his new phone. He settled on the sofa along with Ginger and the book of instructions.

An hour later, in perhaps one of the worst tempers he had ever had, he threw his new phone on the floor and growled his fury at Ginger, who took one look at William and made for the toilet window. Once again, William read the manual of instructions on how to make a call. He seized the apple pie woman's booklet yet again and found the advertisement which had attracted his attention before. Patiently, he began to dial, this time remembering to include the local code, also pressing the icon which claimed to start up the call. This time it worked. Perfect Patios answered. "How may I help you?"

Relieved and triumphant, William shouted, "I want the garden done!"

"Yes Sir?" said the startled lady at the other end of the phone. "No need to shout Sir. What was the name?"

Somehow William restrained himself, spoke in a reasonable tone and got through the ensuing conversation without becoming embroiled in one of his unfortunate misunderstandings. He gave his name and address and arranged for one Ed Smithers to come and inspect the property the next day at 10 o'clock. He even remembered to press the icon which finished the call. Exhausted after this technological struggle he realised he needed a drink like never before and made for the kitchen.

When he returned he drank his lager as if his life depended on it. Mobile phones! He seemed to remember there was something about charging the thing up or it wouldn't work. Surely it wouldn't give up the ghost after just one call? He was about to set it up to charge when he suddenly thought, well nobody knows I've got one, so they can't phone me anyway. And I'm not going through all that again in a hurry to make more calls. So he left it, for the time being, although he didn't turn it off. He wasn't sure how you did that. It was one of the many features he had not mastered.

At this point, he thought about his computer. How simple it seemed after a mobile phone. He switched it on and opened up his emails. There was one from God again!

Here we go, he thought. More daft directives I bet. Still, the old boy has been pretty helpful, really. Now what?

The email said:

Plan ahead. Keep calm. Be yourself. See clearly.

He read and reread this brief missive several times. The Almighty didn't seem too interested in his query regarding his ferreting out what had happened in the past. 'Plan ahead'? Well, that could mean anything from working out what to do next Tuesday or booking a holiday in foreign parts, couldn't it? He most definitely didn't want to do that. The idea of not being able to make himself understood somewhere filled him with horror. He had enough trouble with English-speaking people as it was. He did not want to go abroad. He did not rate abroad. Perhaps he had been there, he thought, in the days when, and hadn't enjoyed it. Planning ahead would have to reveal itself some other way, he thought.

'Keep calm'. Yes, he knew in his heart of hearts what the Top Guy was getting at. His sudden bursts of temper. His awful rages. He should make an effort. Definitely. He would try. 'Be yourself'. Well, who else could he be? That was a daft directive if ever there was one. 'See clearly'. Well he wore glasses, now and then; mostly he lost them and spent a lot of time looking for them. Of course he wanted to see clearly. The glasses helped him to see clearly. What else could it mean? A small shoot of anger threatened to swell up inside. I haven't got time for all this nonsense, he thought.

He was also disappointed. Sometimes the messages had made him very angry, but it had all come clear in time. This time he just didn't understand it. Was he supposed to ask the Social people about the past or not? The problem wasn't solved, so he shrugged his shoulders and temporarily forgot about it. He settled down for a prolonged afternoon sleep; his life seemed to have become more exciting and interesting of late, he thought. Perhaps he had God to thank for that but it was certainly tiring. Ginger joined him and they enjoyed a comfortable doze on the sofa.

Later, he and his umbrella went to the pub and again had a pleasant session. Jimmy was there and had to be filled in with the police episode and William recruited several people to help him with his mobile phone, which was just as well as he had apparently set the alarm to go off at 3 a.m. Choosing which ringtone he preferred occupied most of the regulars for at least half an hour but he got the hang of it all after a while. He even found out how to switch it off. There were one or two games on his phone which intrigued him, but it was disappointing he couldn't take pictures. Up until now he had no idea that people could take pictures with their phones, anyway, but to find that he was one of those who couldn't annoyed him but there it was. At least he could phone people now.

He came home very pleased with life in general, slightly tipsy but not as much as usual, went to bed and slept well.

The next morning he made a good substantial breakfast, which Ginger joined in with appreciatively, and decided to go and buy a paper, as he wanted to catch up on what had happened in the scandals he had been reading about. However, before he could do that, Ed Smithers turned up to look at the garden.

"How much do you want done Mr. Penfold?"

"All of it," said William. He was in no mood to haggle over bits and pieces.

"Well, it's not a very big garden, so it wouldn't cost that much. You've already got quite a few large plain slabs outside your kitchen and toilet end of the garden. Do you want herringbone pattern, or to continue the large slabs or crazy paving? I've got pictures here."

William considered the illustrations. "I like the crazy paving," he said firmly.

"Want any more spaces left at the edges for a border or in the middle, for plants?"

"No," he said firmly.

"Well, we'd have to charge you for taking away all the rubbish. There's a lot to clear, you realise. What about the shed?"

"I don't want it. Take it away. And what's inside it."

Ed Smithers fiddled about with his pencil and brochure. "Could do it for £580."

William was shocked. £580 for covering his garden area with concrete! "£250," he said, sticking his chin out belligerently. "There's a proper lawnmower in the shed, and a spade and so on. You'd get all those."

"Not worth anything. Four fifty for plain slab paving," said Ed Smithers, " that's my last word."

"Four hundred," said William. "That's mine."

"Gawd," said Ed. "I'll do it next week. Monday. What's that plank doing there?"

"It's for the cat," explained William.

"You need a cat flap," said Ed. "One of my men'll put one in for you in your back door. Can't have that plank there."

"Alright," said William.

"£420 then," said Ed. "Plus cost of cat flap," he added hastily.

He and William shook hands and William offered him a drink as they went back through the kitchen. William had to give Ed a deposit, which he managed from the £1,000 he still had left from the lorry driver. He put the remainder in his wallet. The conversation seemed to have suited both of them and they parted amicably.

Well, that's going to make a hole in my £1000, thought William. On the other hand, it would solve the garden problem in one go. "You can't take it with you," he said philosophically, as he considered his purchase.

Well satisfied with his morning's encounter, he returned to the front room. Before he could make himself ready to go out, he saw that he had received some post. There were two letters. One was from Denis and Robert, who had sent him a new bus pass and given him a date for their next visit in two weeks' time, which would coincide with the annual review of Mr. Penfold's case. They also warned him that there would shortly be a visit from a Mr. John Forbes from the Psychiatry and Counselling Outreach Department. He would prepare a report of William's case to be considered at the annual review, at which several people would be present from the Social Services. There was also a letter from Mr. Forbes, who said that he would be visiting Mr. Penfold next Friday at 2 o'clock in the afternoon and hoped that would be convenient.

William began to consider his position. He didn't like the sound of the Psychiatric Department. Were they thinking of sending him back to the place with the red curtains? He was getting on quite nicely these days. Yes, he did drink a lot, but nowhere near as much as he used to. He was eating better and looking after himself and Mrs. Brenner's cat. He'd made friends. He'd bought a sugar bowl. He knew he hadn't got on with Denis and Robert as well as he might. They were a bit daft in his opinion but they had tried to be helpful. So long as he didn't tell them about the motor scooter episode and the credit card and money he had found in his jacket they couldn't find anything to complain about, could they?

None of it was his fault. But he would certainly keep quiet about the emails from God. That would put the cat among the pigeons.

The bus pass cheered him up. He wondered what he had done with the previous one. He must have been stupid to get rid of it. Now he could go to the Protect and Save building society place and demand a cheque book. Not that he actually intended to use it, given that that was all he had. Still, you never knew, he felt he ought to have one. And he could track down the dressing gown shop and try to get it into his head where the pharmacy was. He had no idea where his doctor's surgery was, he realised, but then he didn't want to go there.

Also, he suddenly realised, he could go to see Mrs. Brenner, on the hospital bus. He had seen that outside the newsagent's. He could take Ginger in his covered cat carrier. The world was wide open!

That afternoon he walked to the library and from there he discovered where the Community Institute was, more or less next door, where they held all the classes. He went in and found a small queue with the sign 'Enrolment' above them. He'd had a sudden brilliant idea. When it came to his turn he said, quite loudly, "I want to sign up for a class."

"Certainly, Sir. Which class was it?"

"Sculpture in stone."

The signing-up assistant hesitated. One had to be so careful. Classes were open to everyone, of course, but here was an elderly gentleman who seemed to be not so very steady on his feet and who did smell somewhat of alcohol, wanting to join a class that was perhaps a little strenuous for him. Gently she attempted to put these considerations into tactful words and William reacted, as he always did to opposition of any kind, with a furious response. He said he was perfectly capable of hauling bits of stone around and carving it up and he was having his garden specially paved over so that his statues would have a safe home. He could see very clearly (there he paused, as the phrase jolted his memory a bit) and he knew what he was doing, which was more than the Community Institute did. Did they expect him to go to silly things like bridge or line dancing? She explained he would have to manage all sorts of tools, some of which might be dangerous, and there would be dust flying about, which might cause irritation, and your hands had to be very steady indeed. The row began to escalate, as rows do, and a senior person arrived on the scene. He was more adamant and hostile from William's point of view and despite William waving his umbrella and threatening to consult his solicitors about his human rights, he got nowhere.

Eventually he signed on, reluctantly, for cookery, at £50 for 11 weeks, which partially calmed him down. "Only if they know something about artichokes," he snapped at them. The assistant assured him that the teacher knew everything there was to know about artichokes and, with that, he had to be content.

CHAPTER 14

After this disquieting conversation William got on the No. 74, intending to go to the Protect and Save building society. He dutifully showed his bus pass and took a seat. But it was some while before he realised the bus was going in the wrong direction and he was almost out of the town. It was approaching leafy lanes and a huge garden centre on his right before he managed to get off the bus. Swearing to himself he decided to enter the garden centre as it offered a café and cream teas, which he felt he needed. The centre was not his sort of place at all, "Full of bloody plants," he muttered, but he enjoyed the cream tea that he bought in the café. Wandering through this, to him, alien world, he saw a sign directing him towards Statuary and Garden Ornaments. There he entered an area brimful of all sorts of stone creations, everything from garden gnomes to ducks, dogs, cats, meerkats and larger, more original statues.

One in particular attracted his attention. It was taller than he was, 6' to 7', and seemed to be of two figures, though what exactly they were doing was not absolutely clear. One had a raised arm which held a bit of wire or something. The other had a rather twisted foot, though you couldn't be sure whose foot it was. You couldn't really tell where one figure ended and the other began nor even what gender they were. You had to make your own mind up. There was a long piece of red-painted metal going across the middle, almost through the centre of the statuary, though it was difficult to see the relationship of the bar to the rest of the design. William walked round it several times, gazing intently. It was called Night Vision. He couldn't see why it was called Night Vision. He tried to look at their faces but one was half-hidden in some drapery and the other looked quite blank. One of them held a sort of remote control in his or her hand but what that was controlling was not obvious.

I like that, thought William. I really do. If they won't let me make my own statue I'd like that one. I could put that in my paved-over garden. I wonder how much it is.

He asked a garden assistant. The assistant said he would find out. It is possible no-one had ever asked him that before. Mostly people wanted gnomes and ducks and meerkats and things. He came back and told William that the statue was in the sale, as there was a very slight chip on the base, and so it would cost only £110 which was, he assured him, a massive reduction from the original price of £250.

William asked how long it had been for sale and the assistant, who was very young and not the sharpest pencil in the box, replied that it had been for sale for a very long time, for months, actually, and there had been no interest in it, not like the lovely meerkats, would the gentleman like to consider some of the other products?

William, fresh from his triumph with Ed that morning, and spurred on by his anger at being rejected from the sculpture class, was gaining in confidence every minute. He said, "You go back to your manager and offer him £75 for Night Vision." The assistant scuttled off and William sat down on a nearby stone seat to wait for his reply.

Back came the assistant, this time accompanied by the manager. "Good afternoon, Sir. So nice to see someone taking an interest in our fine statue. This is an original piece by a local craftsman. I think my assistant told you about the slight chip on the base, otherwise this really would not be in our sale. I'm afraid £75 is really far below what this is worth."

"Why is it called Night Vision?" inquired William.

"Well, I don't really know," admitted the manager. "Artists see things in a different way," he offered up lamely.

"£110 is far too much for me," said William, as sadly as he could. "Senior citizens see things in a different way, too."

"Oh dear," said the manager, thinking rapidly. The unsellable statue had been there taking up space for far too many months now. "I will come down to £85 but that's all I can do."

William knew when he was beaten. "Alright. £85 it is. But can you deliver it?"

"Certainly, Sir. It will cost £20 though if you live local. We will need two men at least to manage that thing, er, that statue. Are you paying by credit card, Sir?"

"Cash," said William firmly. He still had the rest of the £1,000 in his pocket as he had had to pay Ed a deposit earlier.

So the statue project cost William £105 in all, but he felt relatively satisfied with his purchase. The statue he ordered to be delivered in 10 days' time, as he needed to be sure to have the paving done first.

He caught the No. 74 to go home, stopping off at the Protect and Save, but once again they were closed. He decided to leave it till the two Social people were with him although he did read their opening and closing times carefully before again catching another No. 74 to get him back to the library. Only then did he realise he had forgotten to pinpoint the whereabouts of the dressing gown shop. Never mind, he thought, I've had a very satisfactory day, one way or another.

Ginger was in and met him enthusiastically. William felt, if not on top of the world, at least steady and pleased with his day. Now all he had to get through were these two visits from the psychiatrist man and the review people, which included the two Social men he knew already.

"Two more hurdles to go, Ginger, and we'll be alright." Thursday evening he had a very cautious session in the pub explaining to Jimmy that he needed his wits about him the next day.

Friday dawned. William had been thinking about this meeting all night. What exactly was it for? He must remain on his guard, not give this Forbes person any sort of reason to shove him off to the place with the red curtains. That was the worst that could happen. But there were other possibilities. Supposing he went on about how William would be better off in a Home? He had to show that he was perfectly able to conduct his own satisfactory life by himself. Granted he did need the help of Denis and Robert, or at least one of them, he wasn't sure he would manage the pills and the financial things without them, but by and large he'd get by.

Well, sort of. There must be plenty of people in a worse state than him. He had to prove he wasn't drinking to excess any more. No more total blind-drunk wipe-outs lying on his doorstep, unable to put the key in the lock. Where did that memory come from? he suddenly thought. Was that how he had been?

His mind dwelt on all the awful possibilities and he tried hard to suppress the growing rage inside his head. Keep calm. Be yourself. That's what God had said. The Top Guy knew what he was talking about. Don't pretend, be yourself. But don't mention the Top God.

Anyway, this Mr. Forbes might be as big an idiot as the two Social men; might be someone he could run rings round. After all, he had been an administrative manager, hadn't he? That must have meant he had to manage people. And he must not get into a rage. That was when things went wrong. He promised himself to keep calm.

There was a ring at the door. Forbes was here. He and Ginger went to open the door and let in their visitor, Mr. Forbes. He was a tall man, dressed in a neatly-tailored suit, good shirt, smart tie. He had a direct gaze with a keen, intense, assessing sort of look. William felt instinctively that there would be no running rings round this one.

William, who had on his jacket and a fairly clean T-shirt and his cream trousers, invited his visitor into the front room. There they faced each other, Mr. Forbes on the sofa and William on his computer chair. Mr. Forbes had a blue notebook with him.

"Well, Mr. Penfold – may I call you William? – it's a long time since we met. In fact you may not remember me."

"No, I don't."

"Well, your troubles really overwhelmed you about a year ago and I was instrumental in attempting to sort it all out then. How have you been getting on here?"

"Very well indeed, thank you. I'm alright."

"Are you taking your pills?"

"Yes, well, I don't always get them right. The Social men write it down but I do miss one or two occasionally."

"Where have Denis and Robert written it down?"

It was a simple question but it flummoxed William. He'd used their sheet of instructions to write something down on. What was it? Damn and blast it. Thankfully he remembered at last.

"You're sitting on it," he said at last. "I was making a list. For reference."

Mr. Forbes fished out William's list as he spoke. Oh no, thought William. What did I put on that list? "You must keep this safe and readily to hand, William. It is very important that you take all your medication at the right time." Black mark, thought William, but that's not too bad. He hasn't turned the medication sheet over.

"What about your drinking?"

"Oh, much better, much better. I don't drink nearly as much as I did. Honestly."

"How much per day do you think you drink?"

"Oh, just a few bottles, a pint or two. Perhaps three." Mr. Forbes stared at him. "Or four or five. Depends. Perhaps more, sometimes," he added, weakly. William felt that he wasn't doing very well.

"I've got a cat," he said. "Ginger." Ginger dutifully jumped on the sofa and sat down with his head on Mr. Forbes' knee. "Actually, it's not my cat, it's Mrs. Brenner's."

"Ah, now Denis and Robert tell me you tried to do something in Mrs. Brenner's garden and the police got involved."

"Yes, well, it wasn't my fault, they were so stupid." William launched into a description of the complex events of the day the police took him off to the station. Mr. Forbes listened with raised eyebrows and a patient expression.

"How are you managing for money, William?"

"Oh, yes, well, that's alright, the two Social men sort it out for me, you know."

"Denis tells me you had a little altercation at the bank the last time you went there."

"It was disgraceful." William became angry as he thought about it. "Apparently I've got some money but she wouldn't let me see without my passport and Robert had got the passbook thing so I couldn't have a cheque book."

"Why would you want a cheque book?"

"It's my money, my human rights," announced William, sure of his ground here.

"I see," said Mr. Forbes, making further notes in his little blue notebook. "You were not happy in the pyjama shop, I believe."

"Wasn't I?" The question caught William off balance. "I can't remember that. But they are stupid, these assistants, you know. They don't always understand what you say to them."

"Or the pharmacy." Mr. Forbes was obviously like a terrier that won't let go.

"Can't remember that, either." William wriggled uncomfortably.

He wanted to tell Mr. Forbes he'd been to see Mrs. Brenner in hospital but he suddenly remembered that was when he had had a motor scooter and before he had got a bus pass. So he decided to keep quiet.

"Are you religious, William?"

"No." Best avoid all mention of the Almighty. William wondered what would come next.

"Why did you put your kitchen table in the garden?"

"Can't remember."

"William, is your memory still on the blink? Do you recall anything at all of what happened to you before you came to live here?"

"Not much. Except the red curtains."

"Red curtains?" Mr. Forbes looked startled.

"Someone sent me to a place with red curtains. Where you kept asking me about what I remembered about the past, about the days when, and I said I didn't and couldn't and you wanted me to stop drinking, but I like drinking. I don't want to go there again."

"Ah, I see. Well, you are so much improved, William, I really can't see you being asked to go there again, so I should stop worrying about that." Mr. Forbes smiled.

William felt mightily relieved. Mr. Forbes idly turned over the list that he was holding and studied William's 'for reference' items.

"Well, I believe you have a bus pass now. And you're still interested in getting a cheque book, but I wouldn't touch that money if I were you. Yes, you need a dressing gown, good idea; what money are you thinking about, William? Your account money I suppose. Leave it alone, if you can. Your garden is a bit of a mess, I agree, just have to tidy it up if possible. What's this about a booklet and an apple pie woman?"

William breathed again. Mr. Forbes had unknowingly skated over the difficult questions. He explained about Mrs. Watson and the apple pie and her suggestion of line dancing and said he preferred cookery because he wanted to know how to cook artichokes. Mr. Forbes stared at him over that, but seemed to accept it.

"A telephone would be a bit expensive and unless you can control these outbursts of anger it won't work, William. That's why it is not recommended for you. Not after what happened before."

"Why, what happened before?" William spoke belligerently and Mr. Forbes stiffened up, expecting an outburst right now.

"You made some very rude and aggressive phone calls you know. It led to a lot of trouble."

"Well, I wouldn't now," said William, without giving away the fact that he had actually got a phone now.

Mr. Forbes thought for a while. "Well, I must say that the picture is better now, although there are a few worries, perhaps about money and memory. Your benefits seem to be keeping you going at the moment. I will think things over and will join the others at your annual review. Is there anything you would like to ask me?"

William looked at him and thought hard.

"Yes, why am I here?"

Mr. Forbes sighed. "Well, this is not the ideal place for you I must admit, but it's all the council had when you turned up. A house is not the best place for you and perhaps a modern flat would have been better. Do you want to put in for a change?"

Alarmed, William said, "Oh no, that's not what I meant. Actually, I quite like it here now. I've got friends." He puffed himself up as he said this. He recalled Mrs. Brenner referring to him as 'my friend' and Mrs. Watson, the apple pie woman, Mrs. Jenkins and all the people in the pub. "No, I don't want to move. I just wanted to know about – about my life. About the days when. I think I could deal with it now."

"I see." Mr. Forbes seemed deep in thought. "William, I think we will defer that discussion till you have your review. At the review there will be several people you know and who have helped you along in the recent past. We shall have to decide how much support you now need, whether it is more or less than you are currently having. And that seems like a good time to address your queries about what happened in the past that has caused you problems now. I look forward to seeing you at your review."

William, unnaturally subdued, offered Mr. Forbes a cup of tea, which he declined, and then showed him out.

"Thank God that's over, Ginger," he said, "like being in front of the Head at school. Tell you what, let's have a long, long drink. And then, when we've had something to eat, I'm going to have another one. Is there any of that apple pie left? And then I shall go to the pub and there I shall have several more, whatever. And if they have to carry me home, too bad."

They didn't have to carry William home, but it came pretty close. A couple of men, Bill Watson and a mate of his, kept him pretty well upright until he reached his own front door; when he got inside he made for the sofa and stayed there until half-past nine the next morning. There was no way he could have got up the stairs. "That's what a dose of psychiatry does for you, Ginger," he muttered, as he fell onto the sofa, "sends you round to the pub quicker than anything." Then he passed out.

CHAPTER 15

Next day, he suffered from perhaps the worst hangover he had ever had. Ginger despaired of ever being fed and rummaged round the kitchen to find something edible. Late morning, Maisie Watson, having heard from her husband of William's excessive drinking the previous night, turned up with some nice light soup and crusty bread, which he could just about manage and was very grateful for. She inquired if he had signed up for the line dancing and was disappointed to be told no. She was interested to hear that he had agreed to go to the cookery class though, and added it to her list of confirmatory facts about poor William and his hard life.

He took it easy that Saturday but decided he would go to see Mrs. Brenner again on the hospital bus on Sunday. He knew of the bus as he had seen it starting from outside the newsagent's. It would be easier for him with Ginger in his carrying case, without the problem of the umbrella and the parking. He could try to explain about the gardening enterprise which had gone so badly wrong. He wouldn't like her to come home and just be faced with what he had managed to do to her prized garden. Also, he wasn't sure what was going to happen with Ginger when she came home. Would the cat automatically return to his previous home? To his surprise, he realised he would find that rather upsetting. But if the cat stayed with him and refused to go back to Mrs. Brenner's it would be equally difficult. He remembered too that he had agreed to install and pay for a cat flap from Ed. He wasn't used to pondering such subtle problematic issues and he set off on Sunday in rather a bad mood.

Arriving at the hospital, he felt like a knowledgeable old hand, going directly to the lift and getting out at Acute Admissions. He went straight into the ward and into the small side room where he had found her before. She wasn't there! Only a large and formidable lady with a bandaged leg was facing him, seated on a wheelchair.

"Who are you? Go away," she shouted, pulling her alarm cord. When a nurse came running in she pointed at William and said, "What is this man doing in here? I never asked him in, I don't know him." She was waving her arms about and getting very excited.

"Just a mistake," said William, "where's Mrs. Brenner?"

"Just next door in the small ward. There there, Mrs. Davis, no need to get all worked up. We had a very silly man in here not long ago, with a big umbrella and would you believe it a cat or something, but he's not here now." The nurse continued to calm her patient and William backed out hastily. He didn't care to hear himself described as a very silly man, but this was not the time to have an argument, he could see. He went into the small four-bedded ward next door. Mrs. Brenner was there, dressed, and sitting in an upright armchair. There were three other ladies, two of whom were also seated, looking rather glum in their chairs; the other one was an Asian lady who was lying in bed.

"William Penfold! Oh, how lovely to see you! Have you brought Sandy? Bring up a chair and come and sit down."

William found a spare chair and sat down opposite Mrs. Brenner. Now he was here he wasn't sure how to express himself, especially as the other ladies in the room were all interested to hear what Mrs. Brenner's visitor had to say. "Well, it's about Ginger – I know you call him Sandy – that I've come here. Oh, and the garden. I'm sorry about the garden, I was trying to do my best but the police behaved very badly and it does all look a bit patchy here and there, but Denis said it would all grow back. Here's Sandy. I don't think I'd better let him out here, that nurse was an absolute idiot last time I came." He took the carrying cloth off Ginger's case as he was speaking.

Mrs. Brenner wasn't really listening. Her eyes were fixed on the cat and she reached forward to stroke him between the bars. "Oh, thank you, William, I've missed him so much. I never thought you'd be so kind. Mr. Penfold took it on himself to look after my cat," she said, addressing the other ladies in the room. "Wasn't that nice of him?" The other ladies agreed that it was indeed very nice, and said it was a blessing to have a good neighbour and you didn't get much of that these days. They said Ginger looked very well and Mrs. Brenner had nothing to worry about. One of them said, "Quick, the prison guard is coming back, hide the cat," and William put the carrying cloth back on as fast as he could. The prison guard nurse came in with her blood pressure machine and they all fell quiet.

"What's that about the garden?" asked Mrs. Brenner when the prison guard nurse had gone. William repeated his rather confused explanation, but Mrs. Brenner interrupted him. "I've heard all about it from Maisie Watson," she said. "She came to see me the other day. Don't you worry. I'll sort it out, or get it sorted out, when I get home. I'm coming home soon, you know. You shouldn't be doing gardens, you're not strong enough. You need some proper food. Did you get an apple pie from Maisie? She's good with pies, is Maisie. She's a good cook. Has to be with that husband of hers. Hollow, he is."

William was relieved. "How do you think Ginger will be when you get back?"

"What do you mean? He'll be glad to have his old life back, I expect," she said, surprised.

"Well, I was just wondering, he's used to coming in to me and sleeping there and he's got a cat flap," (William thought it best to make the cat flap a reality to save some explanations about Perfect Patios etc), "and I thought that might, well, upset you. If he went on doing that, I mean."

William had never, at least in recent times, made such a sensitive speech, especially to a woman.

But Mrs. Brenner was made of sterner stuff. "We may have to share him then." And she smiled.

"Righto." He was relieved. " Have a beer," said William. He'd brought two or three bottles of beer in with him, naturally, and felt duty bound to offer one to Mrs. Brenner, seeing as she was being so sensible.

"Well," said Mrs Brenner, "Maisie Watson brought in some lemonade for me, so I could have a small shandy. Would you do that for me, William?"

"Certainly," said William. He made a shandy for Mrs. Brenner, courteously inquiring if any of the other ladies would like one. Two of them did and they emptied their water glasses and William filled them up with shandy. The other lady, who had refused as she was Muslim and didn't take alcohol, found a delicious bag of homemade biscuits and small cakes, which she offered to the group, so they all went to sit round her bed. The afternoon passed very pleasantly and in fact William got through his three bottles of beer and Mrs. Brenner's bottle of lemonade, making shandies for them all, except the Asian lady, who refused all their offers. They became quite merry and talkative and time slipped by. The tea trolley came in and the tea lady was quite surprised that she had no takers but the ladies, who were not stupid, said they were quite content with the Coca Cola Mr. Penfold had brought in for them.

Eventually, William got up to go and Mrs. Brenner had a last stroke of her cat, who had been very quiet during all the talking. All the other ladies also wanted to stroke him and to shake hands with William and he felt he was a great social success. He slipped the cover onto Ginger's carrying case and went to catch the bus, with Mrs. Brenner's profound thanks ringing in his ears.

"Well, that went off very well," said William, when they reached home. "I've got a nice bit of fish for tonight. You'll enjoy that, Ginger. Then it's the pub for me. Perfect Patios tomorrow. That should be interesting. You won't like them, I'm afraid, but they're going to put in a cat flap for you before they go."

The men came at 8 o'clock, which was a shock to William's system. Or rather Ed was, having sent his van round the back into the alleyway. He hammered very loudly on the door – obviously he didn't do doorbells – and woke William and Ginger up and possibly all the nearby householders.

William crawled out of his bed and again cursed the fact that he didn't have a dressing gown. He let Ed in and they went down the garden to open up the alleyway door. "It's all yours," he said and left them to start their work.

It took them most of the morning to clear the garden of litter and rubbish and all afternoon to remove the shed and its contents. But eventually they began to prepare the ground for the laying of the large plain slabs. Ginger's plank was removed, leaving him plainly puzzled as to how to get in, and William had to go outside and call him in. One of Ed's men, Frank, knocked at the back door and asked if William had the cat flap he was supposed to install or did William want him to get it? William didn't have it and had no idea where one bought a cat flap so delegated this to Frank, who said he would bring one the next day.

Despite all the clamour and mayhem in the garden William remained relatively calm. He hadn't realised about workmen and tea or coffee and Ed had to practically ask for it before it dawned on him what was expected. That it might have to be provided twice a day was an even greater shock and he watched carefully from the kitchen window in case they ran over the ten minutes he was mentally allocating them.

The installation of the cat flap caused more trouble than the paving of the garden. William and Frank between them spent over half an hour pushing Ginger through one way and then pushing him back the other but the cat was curiously unhelpful. He obviously wanted his own personal plank, as before, but they persevered and when he had eventually mastered it once, they decided to leave it at that and hope.

Two days later William paid Ed in his kitchen whilst looking out onto a perfectly plain, clean surface, with not a plant or bit of greenery in sight.

"Very nice," he said, liking his minimalist area.

"You could put pots and tubs on it," suggested Ed.

"What for?"

"Well, for a bit of colour. Wouldn't look so…grey."

"I like it grey," said William. "That's my idea of a garden. You can put other things on it beside tubs and pots."

"Such as?"

But William wasn't telling.

He spent a lot of time looking at his nice, new, clean and tidy garden area. It occurred to him that it might be pleasant to have a table and chair outside. A small table and just one chair. So that he could sit outside and regard his statue. He wondered where he could get one. He didn't want to have to go back to the garden centre. He didn't want a posh table. Just an ordinary everyday sort of small table, which you could put a pint of beer on and a plate of chips or something. Perhaps there would be a charity shop on the high street, if he were to get a No. 74 again, one that sold bits of furniture.

So that was three things he had to see to − a small table and chair, a dressing gown and a cheque book. My life seems to be a series of lists these days, he thought. Well, better to have something to do than nothing, I suppose.

There was a bang in the kitchen. It was Ginger using his new cat flap. It certainly made a noise, which William hadn't been expecting, but it was quite useful really; he would always be aware that the cat was actually foraging in the kitchen for anything left about on the table.

All in all he was pleased. If he could get through this Review, which he remembered was Annual, he'd be safe for a year. They might tell him a few things about the days when. It would be up to him to decide if that upset him and set him off like he was before all this Top God stuff started, or if it settled his mind somehow.

He thought about his last message from the Top God. He'd planned ahead alright. He was going to cookery class in September. Not that he was too thrilled about that, he wanted to do sculpture in stone but they wouldn't let him. He'd been angry but not too angry. Perhaps he had realised something of what they were saying. He'd kept calm. Well, not calm but he hadn't given way to the explosive belligerent fury of previous altercations. It was a start, anyway. He still wasn't clear about 'Be Yourself' and 'See Clearly'.

The next few days passed peacefully enough. He showed his new paved garden to Maisie, when she brought a steak and kidney pudding round one day, and she was, as she put it, gobsmacked. "I don't know what Phyllis will make of it," she said, sounding rather anxious.

"Phyllis?" inquired William.

"Mrs. Brenner. She likes gardens."

"Oh, yes. But she might like this. It's… restful."

"Restful? I dunno about that. It's different."

"Do you know where I could get a small table from? Just a little one. And a chair?"

"I don't know. I'll ask around. It would improve it, in my opinion."

The day after this conversation, as he was turning into his street after a visit to the mini-market for beer and sausages, he saw the local hospital patients' bus depositing Mrs. Brenner outside her house. Maisie was with her, carrying her bag and helping her inside. Things were back to normal, then. Would he see Ginger again? He hurried down his street and got to his own front door. When he opened it there was Ginger, eagerly awaiting the sausages, no doubt, unaware that his rightful owner had returned.

William prepared a slap-up meal for the cat and watched him disappear out of the cat flap a little sadly. The afternoon passed by and he ate a solitary meal before going off to the pub. He went a little late this evening but there was no sign of Ginger.

His evening in the pub was somewhat mournful and he drank to try to chase the blues away but they didn't go away and he was swaying badly as he entered his house. At the end of the evening, Ginger was there, waiting for him in the hallway.

"Well, hello," he said, as Ginger miaowed a greeting, "long time no see." Ginger didn't seem hungry for once and they went into the sitting room together. Later they went upstairs to the front bedroom. William got into bed and Ginger curled up on top of the duvet.

"That's better," said William, and fell asleep almost at once.

In the next few days, it seemed that Ginger had himself decided that he would split his time between William and Mrs. Brenner. William would always see him at some point but when the cat would appear he didn't know. He just heard the cat flap bang and knew his small companion would present himself for a greeting and possibly some food. It seemed a satisfactory arrangement to all concerned.

William wondered if he should call on Mrs. Brenner. Did the social conventions require this? She might have taken one look at her battered garden and lost all faith in her neighbour. Maybe he was no longer a welcome visitor. He worried about this, but in the end he decided to stop being so silly, put on his best trousers, jacket and baseball cap and knocked on her door.

CHAPTER 16

"Well, if it isn't William," she said, opening the door wide. "Come on in, I'm just making a cup of tea."

William entered what was in effect a different world. Her house was of course the carbon copy of his, but in reverse. It was also immaculate, tidy, clean and well-decorated with close-patterned wallpaper. There were shelves, photographs, cushions, furniture, plants in fancy holders. True, it was the home of an elderly lady but it was definitely a home. He thought of his own house, ramshackle, messy and rather grubby. What a contrast!

"I've been wanting to thank you for all you did for my Sandy. Now please sit down, I'll go and get the tea things."

He imagined her kitchen. Clean and sparkling, everything just in the right place. She probably had a separate drawer for tea towels and things and bowls and brushes for everything. She came back in to the room bearing a tray. Ginger came with her.

Ginger was delighted to see him and came over for a fuss. They talked about the cat and Maisie Watson, about the hospital, about their houses and the council, and it all passed off peacefully enough. She had provided some tempting small cakes and they drank tea and chatted as if they had known each other for years.

William said, "Have you noticed my garden's been paved over?" He asked rather nervously, half expecting a ringing condemnation.

Mrs. Brenner simply said, "It takes all sorts. You do what pleases you. If you can't manage a garden, then paving it is the best thing." She didn't say a word about his unfortunate mismanagement of the hedge and the mowing. He was most impressed.

She is a bit frail, he thought, less sprightly than she used to be.

"How are you now, Mrs. Brenner? That hospital sort you out?"

"Oh, Phyllis, please," she said. "Well, not exactly. I know I said I tripped over the cat but I am a bit tottery now. They were on about getting some carers in and if it gets worse thinking about a Home. I don't want that." She sounded fierce.

"Quite right," said William. "You tell 'em. Do you want any shopping done or anything?" he heard himself ask, much to his surprise.

"That might be very useful, thank you." Mrs. Brenner also asked him about where he got the cat flap from as she thought it would be best for Sandy in her house, too. He said he would give her the phone number of Perfect Patios and also, and here he swelled with pride, his own number in case she needed any help any time. They parted on very good terms and William was very relieved.

When he got home, he reflected on the differences between the two houses. Was it just that Phyllis was a woman and knew about these things? Or had he let everything go so that he lived just on the edge of acceptable? It doesn't have to be in this sort of mess, he thought, looking round his front room and kitchen. Still, it was his home. It was an expression of himself, he thought. He didn't need lots of fiddly little shelves and plants and photos, but it should be cleaner and more comfortable. He could improve it all, given some time. And a bit of money.

The days passed by. He went to the bank on the No. 74 bus and this time he asked for a cheque book, which they said they would send him in the post. After that he found the dressing gown shop, where he bought another pair of pyjamas and a dressing gown. All of this was accomplished without a single argument with anybody and he was very pleased with himself. In a charity shop he managed to find a small round garden table and chair for £10 which would suit him very well. It was a bit battered but still sound and they offered to deliver them the next day for £5.

He thought a lot about the Top God. He must send him a 'thank you' email. But he had to get this review over with. He was actually very worried about the review. What would that Forbes man say? Had he made the wrong impression on Mr. Forbes? How come his future seemed to lie in the hands of these people? They could decide anything. They had such power. Over him and over Mrs. Brenner. It wasn't right but he couldn't fight it. He supposed they were doing their best, in their own way.

He also thought about his brief fling with a motor scooter.

So far, nobody had mentioned it. He hadn't had it very long, of course, and he really hadn't known any of the neighbours at that time, but it worried him slightly. He decided that if challenged he would say it hadn't suited him and he had got rid of it. Maybe he had had one 'on trial'. Yes, that would suit. He'd had one on trial and he hadn't liked it.

The day came for the delivery of the statue. William was full of anticipation and excitement. When the doorbell went he and Ginger, who had come in for some extra breakfast, hurried to the front door. But it was only the table and chair from the charity shop. They looked very homely on his paved back garden area.

"I shall have my breakfast out here, Ginger," he informed the cat. But setting up his meal outside made him realise that he had to carry all the things out that he required. "Bloody nuisance how one thing leads to another," he muttered. "Now I've got to buy a tray."

Later, the statue, in a big van, arrived. William directed it to the alleyway at the back. Various neighbours watched with great curiosity and, as it was hauled out of the back of the van and on to a large trolley, with great amazement, as Night Vision made its appearance.

It stood, big and uncompromising, on the large, plain slabs. There was the upraised arm, the fist clutching bits of wire or flex, there was the twisted foot, there were the two merged figures, one holding a remote control. The colour of the stone seemed to change with the sunshine, sometimes there was a hint of blue, sometimes a pale yellow. William had the statue facing him so that he could see the bright blood-red bar that crossed the statue in the middle. He had it placed centrally in his garden. There was no way you could miss it. Not that he wanted to miss it. He thought it was wonderful. Nothing had pleased him so much for – well, years.

Neighbours looked down with disbelief from their upstairs windows. Some tall ones peered over the fence at the bottom of William's garden. One man lifted up his little boy to have a good look. "What's it look like?" he asked his little boy.

"Well, it's a bit like two Daleks and one of 'ems got a bad foot," he said. "It's really good, Dad."

Maisie Watson arrived bearing a cherry pie and an expression of consuming curiosity.

Confronted by the statue, which she was shown by a very proud William, she was speechless. "What is it called?" asked Maisie, that being the only thing she could think of to say.

"Night Vision," said William.

"Why?"

"No idea," he said, a bit reluctantly. "Artists have their own way of looking at things you know."

"It's a bit scary, I think. What's the remote control thing for?"

"I don't know."

"Let's hope it doesn't start the whole thing up."

William thought that was funny and he burst out laughing, which was something he hadn't done for a very long time.

Later, Mrs. Brenner came in, bearing a large pot of geraniums for William's desert of a garden. When she saw the statue, she had to sit down on William's new chair and put the pot on the table as she stared open-mouthed at Night Vision.

"Well, William, you are a one!" was her considered verdict,

after much thought. "Never thought you were so..." she struggled for an appropriate word, "artistic."

Many of William's neighbours found an excuse to call on him in the next few days to see the statue as news of Mr. Penfold's extraordinary launch into the post-modern art world became generally known. The local newspaper sent a reporter to take photos; they tried to track down the sculptor without success, so made do with a photo of William beaming happily by the side of his new possession.

His public standing was further enhanced by the statue. Already a local hero, on account of his brush with the police, he now became an accepted artistic expert and he was asked to judge the Sculpture and Crafts Exhibition entrants at the local Summer Show. For doing this they actually gave him £20, which pleased him enormously. He gave the top prize to someone who had done a course at the Community Institute in sculpture in stone and produced a small statue of a dog with five legs which William thought was rather good.

CHAPTER 18

A letter came from Mr. Forbes, announcing the date of William's annual review. It was next Friday at 10 a.m. Again, he had a moderate evening at the pub, just in case, and tidied up his house as best he could. He tried to catch up on his pills and took rather a large quantity of them all on Thursday, but they really had very little effect apart from making him a bit dizzy for half an hour.

Anxiously, he let them all in at 10 o'clock. Mr. Forbes, Denis, Robert, another gentleman, a Mr. Travers, and two ladies, Mrs. Wells and Ms. Foster. He had no idea who they were but they seemed to know him, and he ushered them into his front room.

He didn't have seven chairs. There were four seats in the front room, two on the sofa, his computer chair, and another rickety old thing. There was a chair in the kitchen and the new chair in the garden, six in all. Well, they would all have to manage as best they could. They'd all got legs, hadn't they? And he hadn't invited them after all. They'd invited themselves. He'd try to put the lightest one on the rickety chair.

They arranged themselves round the room with William sitting on the arm of the sofa. He thought about tea or coffee, but he didn't have anything like seven cups or mugs, not clean, anyway. So he decided against it.

The meeting got under way. First, Mr. Forbes said that he felt that Mr. Penfold had made enormous progress since a year ago. Mr. Penfold had first come to the attention of the Social Services about a year ago, when it became clear that he could no longer look after himself safely and was causing something of a disturbance in the locality. He had had a spell in The Four Oaks Psychological Clinic to help him with his drink and memory problems and he had stayed in the Rehabilitation Section, which had eventually placed him with the Local Authority in accommodation at his current address. This was not regarded as the proper place for him, but it was all that was available at the time. Here he was assisted by two support workers on a regular basis, who did not offer personal grooming but did otherwise assist with shopping, laundry and visits to the doctor etc.

Mr. Forbes felt that Four Oaks had no more to offer Mr. Penfold although Mr. Penfold himself had expressed the desire to discover more about his past history and it was possible they could assist with that. At the moment, the chief concern was how much help at home did they all feel that Mr. Penfold needed and the views of Denis and Robert would be vital in establishing that and, in addition, how was Mr. Penfold doing socially in relation to other people? All the views of those present, including of course Mr.Penfold, would govern how things were to be set up.

William, feeling Mr. Forbes had gone on long enough,

although he hadn't said anything disagreeable, interrupted the proceedings with an abrupt question, which was, "How old am I? I'd like to know, please."

There was much rustling of papers and searching for information. "69,"said Mrs.Wells, brightly. "Actually, you are 70 on August 14th, that's next Wednesday, William."

"Well, I didn't know that," said William. "It was rather awkward when I wanted to get a bus pass."

"You've got one now," said Denis. "I sent it to you."

"Yes," said William, "but I need to know where all the buses go, don't I? I wanted to go to the high street to see the Protect and Save people, not that they are very helpful, they wanted to see my passport you know, when all I wanted was a cheque book, that was something else I didn't know about, I had another account apparently, anyway the bus went miles in the other direction but that's alright because now I've got Night Vision, which I wouldn't have otherwise and everyone's very pleased with it."

"Night Vision?" inquired at least three of the people at the meeting.

"It's in the garden," said William. "Come and see." William appeared to have taken charge of the meeting.

Somewhat bemused, the group struggled to their feet and, exchanging questioning looks, they all trooped out through the kitchen and into the garden. There they stared in disbelief at Night Vision.

Mr. Forbes made some more notes in the blue notebook, which had made a reappearance.

"You *chose* this?" said Ms. Foster, faintly.

"Yes," said William proudly. "It was in a sale. It's got a

chip on the base. Phyllis gave me those red things," he added, noticing that Mrs. Wells was examining the plant pot which had geraniums in it on the table.

"Who is Phyllis?" asked Mr. Travers.

"Next door," said William. "She's not the apple pie lady, that's Maisie. But she's very nice. She owns Ginger really."

"Ginger is the cat," explained Robert, feeling that he had to interject before it all got too complicated.

"Let us resume the meeting," said Mr. Forbes, rather pompously. They turned and trudged back to the front room.

When they were all settled again he asked Denis and Robert to give their views on how they thought Mr. Penfold should or could manage in future.

Denis said that Mr. Penfold had continued to show signs of aggressive and difficult behaviour in various places but that had dwindled down a bit since the incident with the police. He seemed fit and able, even when drinking, but the main problem was managing his money and he would soon get through the remaining money in his account, now that he had taken charge of it. He was more rational than he had been at the beginning of their acquaintance. He needed help with prescriptions, doctor's appointments, laundry and especially with his money, benefits and bills etc. Perhaps it would be a good idea if he could get his own washing machine. He really did not seem to need two carers, just one, so long as the situation did not deteriorate. He did need help with benefits and bills and so on. His drinking continued but not on anything like the scale that he was engaging in before, but they needed to keep a careful eye on it.

Mr. Forbes agreed with this. One carer once a month,

with guidance about money and benefits, plus emphasis on his medication, would hopefully see him through. He had a small concern about the statue and, he dimly realised, the paving that had been done but Mr. Penfold had very little money, all told, which would not last long in any case. Why shouldn't he spend it as he wished?

William took a deep breath. "What about the past?"

Mr. Travers and Mrs. Wells looked at each other.

"What do you want to know, William?"

"I want to know what happened in the days when," said William firmly.

There was a pause. Mr. Forbes said, "William, I am not sure that you really want to know all the ins and outs of the past. What I am going to suggest is that Mr. Travers and Mrs. Wells give you a brief outline of what brought you here and then, if you want a detailed recounting of your previous life, that you make an appointment to come to the Rehabilitation Centre…"

"That's the place with the red curtains?" interrupted William.

"Yes," said Mr Forbes.

"Right, well, fire away," ordered William.

Mrs. Wells spoke. "When you first came to us at Four Oaks Rehabilitation, William, you were in a dreadful state. It seems that many years ago your wife left you and the flat you shared had to be sold as part of the divorce. There were no children. You then purchased a different flat, not quite as good as your previous one. Your job as administrative manager at a shoe Factory did not go well and eventually you were made redundant. You were without a job for a long time and you lost what money you had left by investing rather badly and by drinking too much. Your flat was repossessed by the mortgage company and you moved into a bedsit in rather a seedy area. You continued to drink too much. Your aggressive conduct got you into trouble, both face to face and on the phone. Eventually you were unable to look after yourself and often had to be picked up off the street. We took you in and tried to help you and restore you to some semblance of normal living as we felt that we could begin to start a rejuvenating process. Your Local Authority and Social Services suggested that we try to help you live in your own home again. That is an outline of the story which you felt you could not begin to remember and did not want to remember."

William stood silent. So that was the answer to the days when. They hadn't been so grand after all. He had to balance that against what he had now. A council house in a bit of a tip, some recently made friends, a half-share in a cat, and an interesting statue, plus some help with sorting out money and medication. So, all in all, he wasn't doing too badly these days.

The meeting watched him. Would there be an explosion? Or a breakdown? Or a silent acceptance?

Quietly, with dignity, he said, "Thank you all very much. If I need to know more I'll be in touch. When are you coming again, Denis, I think I need to get a washing machine, don't you?"

"I think we'll be off now, William. I hope you're satisfied with what we have established?" said Mr. Forbes. "We'll see you next year, hopefully. Keep the drinking down."

They all trooped out. William went to the kitchen and fixed himself a drink. He had a lot of thinking to do, but

Ginger was of the opinion he had a lot of eating to do, and made his preferences known. They settled down together in the front room. William fell asleep, exhausted with the worry of the meeting and the results of his questions.

Later, he went to the pub, in a quieter, more thoughtful mood than usual. Bill Watson asked him what was up and he replied that he was growing old and didn't like it. He would be 70 next Wednesday. He buried his face in his beer and slammed it down on the table.

Bill studied him intently. "William, what is 70? It's the new 57, innit? It's nothing. Look at you. I've seen you perk up no end, you know. You walk straighter now than you did and if you keep this up you can have a full life for the next twenty years or so. I reckon you've had a bit of a going-over, one way or another. I think you're due a birthday party. We'll all be there, 7 o'clock on Wednesday. Hear that, lads?" he said to the small group at the table. And so it was agreed. The street was going to turn up at William's, with something to eat and something to drink and they would all drink a toast to William and the Dalek, as the statue was called locally.

Later that night, William sat in front of his computer, trying to work out what sort of mood he had been in when he first got in touch with the Top God. How desperate, how angry he must have been. How he had longed for – what was it? Ah, yes. Serene comfort. Now, these days, that was what he had found. Well, of a sort. He was as near to serene comfort as he was ever going to get. He needed to find the words to say thank you, to express his gratitude – yet where had the ideas, the strange solutions come from? It was as if they had always been there, within himself. Slowly, he nodded to himself. Yes.

They had always been there. This mysterious Top God had drawn them out of him. He knew now that he need not fear 'in the days when'. Nor did he need to think that things were better 'in the days when'. That wasn't true. They weren't. All that belonged to a different life – that was then, this is now. He didn't need to find out more. He knew enough to know he wasn't going back to the days when. He wondered, briefly, if he had any family of any kind. Did he have relatives of any kind? Were they still alive? No. Sod the days when. Been there. Done that. He was himself. On his own, but alright.

And, he remembered, I've got a birthday coming up!

He opened up his emails. He wanted to say 'thank You, thank You, thank You! I'm doing fine, Your message received and understood'. The list of messages was still there and the last one was still plain and definite but, as he watched, the words seemed to fade to a shimmering misty grey. Within a few seconds they had all gone.

I'm seeing clearly alright, he thought. Night Vision! He laughed.

There were no emails, none of them, all gone as if they'd never been, but he did not grieve at their disappearance. It's been special – utterly, unbelievably special – but nothing lasts for ever. I was lucky to have had them. My special secret. I can manage without them now. My amazing emails!

But two thoughts remained and would not leave him. Could he manage without his special guidance? And, more troubling, who, or what, was this Top God person?

He had a sudden, very clear mental image of a woman with long dark brown hair and creamy skin, staring directly at him. She was very angry and rather defiant. She said, in a definite sort of tone, "Today, William, is the first day of the rest of my life." He heard a door slam. The memory was startlingly clear.

Oh hell, no, he thought. Not that. Not the days when. I can't remember her but she'll come back. I know she will. They're all going to come back and spoil things. I'm not having that. I don't mind knowing what went on if they want to tell me but I'm not going to remember off my own bat. So there!

But it wasn't really clear-cut, was it? Maybe the memory thing was not in his hands to control. Maybe he would need the Top God to help him out, after all.

"Dear God, Ginger," he said. "I don't half need a drink!"

For more information on Josephine Falla,
please visit her website:

www.josephinefalla.co.uk .